# MYSTERY SHORT STORIES FOR KIDS: A COLLECTION OF 20 PUZZLING, MYSTERIOUS DETECTIVE AND WHODUNNIT TALES FOR CHILDREN

TIME TRAVEL, SPY ADVENTURES, MYSTERIOUS INVENTIONS, SPACE EXPLORATION AND MORE

JOHNNY NELSON

SILK PUBLISHING

# CONTENTS

# THE PEOPLE OF ZENUN

The ancient city lay abandoned for centuries. Everything in the city was intact—from the homes of the citizens to the palace.

*If everything is intact, does that mean the people of Zenun disappeared without a trace? Where could they have gone?*

Thoughts began running through my mind. My sister had commented that I couldn't enjoy things without questioning them. Perhaps it's *nothing.*

"Rob! Look what I found!" My sister, Emma, excitedly ran towards me, flashing a rare piece of electronics.

It looked like a phone, but it was built weirdly—I had never seen a phone that looked like it.

"Where did you find it?" I asked her.

"At one of the houses of the people of Zenun." Emma replied.

"So, is that how they used to communicate back in the day?" I asked.

"Maybe, but the phone is still new. If it was from ancient times, wouldn't it be dusty and old?" Emma explained.

"Hmm," I said, stroking my chin.

*Are people still living here? How do they survive without contact from the outside world?*

"Always trying to be the detective! What's on your mind?" Emma asked.

"Nothing important! We are on a field trip, we should enjoy our time here instead of playing 'detective' as you call it!" I said while smiling.

I held Emma's hand, and we joined our school group.

"Where were you? It's almost at night. We are about to leave!" Mr. Sheffield asked angrily.

"Sorry Mr. Sheffield, we were just exploring." Emma replied.

"That should never happen again without my supervision! Do you understand?" Mr. Sheffield said.

"Yes! Sir." Emma and I replied consecutively.

Mr. Sheffield led us out of the temple, and we walked towards the gate.

Emma was still behind, but I looked back after a while, and I didn't see her.

She was my sister, and it was my duty to protect

her. I moved away from the group and went to look for her.

After a few minutes of searching for Emma, I found her.

"Where were you?" I asked shakily, "They are about to close the city, we need to go to the gate area." I insisted.

I held Emma's hand, and the two of us ran as fast as possible, hoping to arrive at the gate on time, but destiny had other plans for us.

As soon as we arrived near the gate, we saw the bus leaving!

The gates were closed as well, and there was no way out of this hauntingly beautiful ancient city of Zenun.

"What should we do? This is your fault!" I lashed out at Emma.

"I'm sorry," Emma replied in a tone that suggested she was honestly sorry.

"What did you go back to the Temple to do?" I asked.

"I forgot the phone and I had to go back." Emma said.

"Why are you fascinated by this place, Emma? Do you feel like something is missing? Or, perhaps the detective in you thinks there's more to this." I asked.

"I know being a detective is your 'thing' but ever since I arrived. I feel as if there's something special about this city. Everyone disappeared without a trace yet everything is still intact. What's more? We found a phone we don't know about." Emma explained.

"What should we do?" I asked.

"Let's find out what's so mysterious about this town." Emma suggested.

"Well, I must admit I had my fair share of doubts about this ancient city as well but I didn't want to get into it." I said. "But, since we are already here, there's no harm in finding out what happened to the people of Zenun." I added.

"Alright! Let's get ready for our adventure! Do you still have your snacks?" Emma asked.

"Yes, I do," I replied.

"Same! Now we won't starve throughout the night. First, let's eat." Emma said.

We went inside a hut, sat in the dining area, removed the snacks from our backpacks, and ate them.

Soon after, darkness began to spread throughout the city.

The moon lent its light to us as we walked throughout the city, trying to find clues about this peculiar ancient place.

Since we found the phone in the Temple, that's where we headed to. As we arrived, we were glad to see the fire lighted up the temple.

As we explored around for clues, a strong voice asked,

"What are you doing in my temple?"

When we looked behind us, we saw a ghost of a man who seemed sorrowful. His chest was empty. It looked as though someone stole a piece of him.

Immediately, we started running, but the ghost followed us anyway.

Once we arrived at the end of an allay, we stopped to catch a break, but the ghost was still behind us.

"Are you here to free my people?" The man asked. "Do not fear, I won't harm you." He insisted.

"Who are you people? Why do they need to be freed?" I gathered an ounce of courage and asked.

"I am King Tshuna II, my people were turned into stone after my son led a rebellion. In exchange he was given eternal life, now he roams outside the walls of Zenun as a high ranking military man." The man replied.

"How can we free you people?" Emma asked.

"By taking the Diamond in the middle of the temple and inserting it into the space in my chest." King Tshuna replied.

"We can't do this! It's too much responsibility. King Tshuna, it was nice to meet you but we have to leave. Is there another door out of the city?" Emma asked.

"The door is at the far end of the temple. I can't force you to help us. If you want to go back to your normal lives, you are free to do so." King Tshuna explained.

"Emma, I want to help!" I said.

"No, we have to go home. It's cold and at night. Mom and dad must be worried." Emma insisted.

"I'm sorry King Tshuna." I said as Emma, and I left.

When we arrived at the gate, we realized we needed keys to open the door, so we went back to ask King Tshuna.

As we arrived at the spot we left the king, we heard footprints behind us.

"Get them!" The man shouted!

It was the rebellious prince. He was a strong military man with influence.

Emma and I ran and hid at a spot in the temple and kept quiet. Well, at least I did because Emma coughed, and that exposed us.

The two military men took us to the rebellious prince, and he asked why we were in the temple late at night.

As much as we tried explaining that the bus had left us and we had just come for a school trip. The prince was convinced we were shapeshifters pretending to be children to free the people of Zenun.

"You think you can play with my intelligence? So many like you have come but they haven't succeeded." He said.

He instructed the men to escort us to the dungeon.

As we arrived, we couldn't help but notice the foul

smell covering the area. There were skeletons on the floor as well.

As the men left, King Tshuna showed up. He gave us the keys to access every part of the temple, and thanks to him, we could escape the dungeon.

In return, Emma and I decided to free his people.

We waited until the men and the prince left and went to the middle of the temple. We took the Diamond and placed it on the chest of King Tshuna.

Suddenly, he came back to life and was a real man again — not a ghost.

We went to the room where the people of Zenun were, and they all turned to real people again.

The whole city was filled with happiness and cheers. Everyone was happy to see their family once again.

As the prince came back, he noticed everything had changed. King Tshuna ordered his arrest and took away his power of eternal life as punishment.

Since the people of Zenun didn't want to be in the spotlight, they told us not to tell anyone about what happened. King Tshuna thanked us for helping his kingdom come back to life.

"King Tshuna, we have one last question. We found this in the temple." Emma said as she gave him the phone. "Did you use this to communicate?" She asked.

"No, that's too old! Our forefathers used that! Instead, we used these centuries ago to communicate."

King Tshuna said as he showed her a touchscreen phone.

"How, how di-di...how did you have that centuries ago? We just made the first touchscreen phone years ago?" Emma's voice shakes as she asks the question.

"Well, the main reason why we were betrayed by our dear prince was because an explorer discovered that we were too ahead of time. Our equipment and buildings were too advanced. Out of fear, they sentenced us to what you freed us from. Thank you." King Tshuna explained.

King Tshuna gave us gifts and sent us back home safely in the wee hours of the night.

As we arrived, our parents were happy to see us. Mother grounded us, but the adventure was worth it.

As we woke up in the morning for breakfast, the newscaster reported that the ancient city of Zenin had disappeared.

Emma and I looked at each other and smiled.

As we opened the gifts, King Tshuna had given us as a token of thanks. We were surprised! He had given us the most advanced technology gadgets! Life would then be a fun ride full of adventures.

# THE LAUGHING VALLEY

It was a beautiful summer day in the Laughing Valley.

The days were always warm and the skies blue—everyone seemed cheerful and content.

Even when things didn't go well, people still smiled since the king had forbidden feeling sadness.

If anyone were caught feeling sorrowful, they would be sentenced to life in the dungeon.

The Kingdom was peculiar because nobody knew if any other places existed because there was no door leading in or out of the Laughing Valley.

In this seemingly colorful kingdom, there lived a special girl called Sade—she could sense something was wrong.

All she ever wanted was to experience life as it was without sugarcoating it.

One day, she gathered courage and asked her mother,

"Mom, what does pain feel like? Have you seen the world beyond this? Is it more beautiful?" Sade asked politely.

Sade's mother smiled and replied, "None of those things exist, sweetie."

"I'll research more about the other side!" Sade tells herself.

The next day as soon as she finished eating her breakfast, she made her way to the older man at sea to ask him more about the kingdom.

"Sade, sometimes, the less you know, the better," The old man at sea says.

Sade sat still in silence. All she wanted was to experience new adventures and feel what she hadn't felt.

Her little mind wandered ever so often; her dreams of a genuine livelihood seemed too good to achieve, but she kept her faith and remained confident in herself.

"Remember, sometimes, things are never as they seem no matter how good they look, " The old man added.

"Why do you say that? What have you seen?" Sade asks eagerly.

"Nothing you haven't yet I'm happy." The older man replies as he laughs hysterically.

"I've made up my mind! I want to see and feel something else." Sade insists.

"You are growing and there's nothing wrong with wanting something different." The older man says.

"I feel as though you are hiding something!" Sade insists.

"What am I hiding, little Sade? Your mind is still as green as grass. You are too young to understand." The older man replies as he laughs.

"Something is off about this kingdom, it feels forced." Sade says.

"With due time little Sade! For now, live your life." He replies as he walks away.

The sun fell away and rested for a while. Sade couldn't sleep that night. All she could think about was finding answers to her questions.

The following day the sun rose and shone brightly, casting golden rays through Sade's bedroom window, waking her up to get ready for the day.

Sade ate her breakfast and went to help her mother at the market.

The day ended pretty quickly, and she went to the sea to look for the older man, hoping he'd give her answers to her questions.

As soon as she sat on the rock, the older man sat beside her.

"Good evening young Sade! What are you thinking about?"

"Something different." She replied.

"Are you sure you don't know anything about

what's beyond *this*?" Sade added while looking at the older man in his eyes.

"You can look for answers from a woman who stays in the far west. She chooses who to meet. You need to make a good impression that will make her try to meet you." The older man replied.

"What's her name?" Sade asked.

"Nobody knows her name but the people nick-named her the red queen because she has tried to make people see they are living in a universe that's far from the truth." The older man replied.

"Thank you, Abdi!" Sade replies.

Sade's excitement took the best of her. She didn't care about the issues outside. She just wanted to experience something different, but the journey to the west was expensive.

In the meantime, she chose to work at the market to save money for the trip.

Seasons passed by, and finally, she had saved the amount of money she needed for the trip.

On a chilly evening, Sade approached her mother.

"Mom, I know the truth." She said,

"What do you mean, my child?" Sade's mother replied.

"We live in a lie." Sade replied.

"We are happy, Sade. What more could we hope for!" Sade's mother said.

"But, it's a lie." Sade insists.

"The world outside *this* is not what you hope for; it's cold and cruel." Sade's mother said.

"What do you know about what lies beyond *this*?" Sade asks.

"Nothing." Sade's mother replies.

At this point, Sade realized she had to find the truth on her own.

Once her mother fell asleep, Sade packed her bags and patiently waited to leave the following day.

She was too excited to get any sleep that night. Finally, she would find the answers to her questions from the red queen.

The following day was gloomy; it felt as though the sky was sad that Sade was going to the West, but that didn't stop her.

In laughing hill, people used hot air balloons to travel long distances.

It was Sade's first time getting on a hot air balloon.

"Is everyone comfortable?" The person controlling the balloon asked.

"Yes," they all replied.

As usual, everyone was happy and cheerful— except Sade. All she wanted were answers.

As the hot air balloon began floating higher and higher, Sade felt excitement rushing through her body.

As the hot air balloon was up in the air. Sade was amazed by the views. The kingdom was so huge that the people below looked like ants—*now imagine seeing the other side of the world!*

After a few hours, they finally landed in the west.

As Sade arrived, she couldn't help but notice this other side wasn't as colorful as home.

Everyone on the other side wasn't overly happy for no reason. Most people were serious throughout the day.

"So, who are you and what are you looking for?" A delicate voice asked.

Sade turned around and saw a woman with eyes as red as fire.

"Sade, I'm looking for the red queen." Sade replied.

The woman started laughing hysterically.

"And what makes you think the red queen wants to see *you*?" She asked.

"Because I'm looking for the truth." Sade replies.

The woman took a close look at Sade and told her to follow her.

"To meet the red queen, you'll have to pass tests." The woman said.

"What tests?" Sade asked.

"Tests to prove you were not sent by the king of laughing hill." The odd woman replied.

"Alright." Sade agreed.

They arrived at a small hut. The unusual woman offered Sade a place to sleep.

"Thanks." Sade said.

"Rest, tomorrow will be a big day!" The woman says as she leaves.

Sade couldn't sleep throughout that night because thoughts ran through her mind.

"What tests did she mean? Will I meet the Red Queen?" She thought.

Soon after, she fell asleep.

The sunset and rose the following day. Sade woke up and sat on the bed. This time, she wasn't feeling happiness. Instead, she felt scared and panicky, an emotion that was new to her.

"You seem scared!" The woman came in and said,

"What's that?" Sade replied.

The odd woman laughs uncontrollably.

"It's an emotion—feeling uneasy." The woman says.

"Oh!" Sade replies.

"The Red Queen would like to meet you." The woman said.

"What about the test?" Sade asked.

"She'll do the test to see if you are worthy." The woman replied.

"Worthy of what?" Sade asks.

"You'll know when the time comes." The woman says.

"Eat your breakfast and I'll take you to her chamber." The woman added.

Sade finished her breakfast, and they all headed to the Red Queen's chamber.

"A young girl? I thought she was a woman." The Red Queen exclaimed.

"Can you provide answers to my questions?" Sade asked.

The Red Queen burst into prolonged laughter.

"I can't deal with children! Send her back home!" The Red Queen said as she left the room.

Sade's heart sank. For the first time, she was experiencing disappointment.

"Wait! Ever since I was born, I knew the world is not what it's supposed to be. Even though I'm young, I've had this hunch for a while." Sade says, hoping it would convince the Red Queen.

"And what is the world supposed to be?" The Red Queen looks back while asking.

"Real." Sade says.

This statement captured the red queen's attention, and she turned around and walked towards Sade.

"How can you know this yet you are merely a child." The Red Queen asks.

"I told you! It's something I have always felt." Sade replies.

"Alright, special child. You passed the test, what do you want to know?" The Red Queen asks as she sits on her throne made of thorns.

"Who are you? Why is this side of the laughing valley so different?" Sade asks.

"It's different because it's *real* as you like to call it.

The other side is simply a fantasy made by scientists to find a way to remove pain from the world. We are stuck in a world with no entry or exit because we are simply lab rats in an experiment. On this side, we know they are watching, we carry everything out with caution and sooner or later we'll leave this illusion for good." The Red Queen explained.

"What is pain?" Sade asks.

"When your mother doesn't understand you, or when you are pricked by a thorn. That's how pain feels." The red queen says.

"So, special child, now that you know, what will you do?" The Red Queen asks.

"Everything in my power to free us all!" Sade says.

After that day, Sade went back home. When she arrived, she realized everything had to change, and as the seasons passed, she grew into a fine freedom fighter, hoping to win the war to return home—wherever that was.

# MAMA!

It was a chilly morning. The cold and wet weather made the day seem a bit kooky—it's as if something unexpected would occur. My mother drove me to school, and I waited for class to begin.

Immediately, the bell rang, and the new science teacher entered the class with the principal.

"Good morning class, this is Ms. Sandoval, she'll be your new substitute teacher." The principal, Mr. Sherlock, explained.

"It's nice to meet all of you, my name is Maria Sandoval and I'll be your science teacher." She added.

Every one started murmuring, "Did you hear what happened to Mrs. Robinson?" My best friend Joanna whispered.

She didn't wait for my response and continued

explaining, "She disappeared during her trip to Hawaii." She added.

"I didn't know!" I whispered.

Even though I wasn't fond of Mrs. Robinson and believed she was an oddball, I still felt terrible about the whole situation.

"Silence!" Mr. Sherlock commanded.

The whole class was immediately filled with utter silence.

"Ms. Sandoval was introducing herself until you rudely interrupted her." Mr. Sherlock added.

"It's fine, I'll take it from here," Ms. Sandoval said as she walked to the center of the class.

Mr. Sherlock walks towards the door and disappears through the corridors.

The lesson was rather interesting even though Ms. Sandoval was a bit kooky—perhaps it's a *thing* among science teachers.

Even though she seemed weird and out of place, I had to admit she was also beautiful.

The bell rang, and it was time for recess. As I walked out of the door, I bumped into Ms. Sandoval, and she helped me collect my stuff.

"Oh no! You don't have to collect my things from the ground." I said.

"Why not?" She asked politely. "It's basic etiquette," She said as she gave me my things and walked away smirking.

What happened was unusual, Mrs. Robinson wasn't kind, but Ms. Sandoval seemed nice.

As I was walking home with Joanna, she began talking about Ms. Sandoval.

"She just moved to our town. I heard she lost a child when she was young and never fully moved on with her life."

"What happened to the child," I asked, sparking an interest so Joanna could talk more about it.

"Well, since she couldn't give birth because her womb was too delicate, the doctors suggested that she should let another woman carry a child for her." Joanna explained.

"Wait! Can someone else carry a child for you?" I asked. I was honestly shocked.

"Yes! It's a *thing* in the world of medicine. We are just too young to know about it but we'll be taught one day." She said,

"Alright, you can tell me more about Ms. Sandoval's baby." I said. I was shocked to hear how interested I was, yet I had just met the woman a few hours ago. She was nice to me, and so I felt terrible for her.

"Nice people go through so much stuff!" I thought.

"Well, once the other woman carried her baby for 9 months, she ran away with the child once it was born, never to be found. Ms. Sandoval is still looking for her missing baby who's now almost our age." Joana explained.

"What a story! I hope Ms. Sandoval finds her child. She seems like a good person," I replied.

"Yes, I agree." Joanna said.

"Where do you find all this *information* about teachers?" I asked.

"A true journalist never reveals her sources." Joanna insisted.

"Alright! I understand, Miss Journalist." I replied.

That evening, we decided to rest at my place until the day ended and Joanna had to go back home.

The following day Joanna was during the weekend. I took my mother to the farmer's market.

Surprisingly, we almost met Ms. Sandoval, and my mother tried as much as possible to avoid her until we entered the car.

I was shocked to see my mother act this way because of a teacher we barely knew.

"What's wrong, mother?" I asked.

"Nothing! She just gave me a weird feeling and I had to leave." My mother explained.

"I like Ms. Sandoval, she's my science teacher and she's really nice." I said.

"I don't like her! Don't be too open or personal with her." My mother insisted.

To make her less panicky, I agreed.

The weekend was fun, and I spent most of it with

Joanna, but it ended pretty quickly, and it was time to go back to school.

As usual, Ms. Sandoval was friendly and offered to tutor me since I was failing in science.

After school, I went to her house, and it was warm and smelled of freshly baked cookies her mother had baked.

"Do you want one *mija* ?" The older woman offered.

"Thank you." I said as I took a piece and threw it in my mouth.

The feeling I experienced while in Ms. Sandoval's house was beautiful—it's as though I had known her and her mother for years.

She tutored me, and we all laughed and enjoyed the evening together. For the first time, I felt truly seen and understood.

It was getting late, so I walked back home.

When I arrived, my mother tried to hide some papers, but I eventually found out they were plane tickets. We would soon move out to another town.

"But why should we move somewhere else!" I asked. " All my friends live here! I also found a teacher I really like which rarely happens." I added, hoping my mother would understand me for the first time.

"I'm tired of this town, it's too crowded. That's all sweetie." She said as she hugged me, but I freed myself and ran upstairs.

*How was I supposed to explain this to Joanna? How could we move? The school year was just getting started! Everything felt off.*

I couldn't sleep a wink that night. The following day, mother explained we were moving the next day, so I had to bid my friends goodbye.

I was still not convinced—something weird was happening. She had been acting suspiciously since she saw Ms. Sandoval.

At school, it was a frenzy of sorrow when I told my friends goodbye. Ms. Sandoval was sad too—the evening we spent together with her mother was memorable.

"I wish you all the best my girl," She said as she hugged me. "I can drive you home," she offered, but I said no to the offer knowing how my mother would react.

When I arrived home, there was a large truck outside, and two men were packing our furniture.

I went to my room and packed everything. Suddenly, I had a knock on the door. It was Ms. Sandoval. I had forgotten my books at her place while she was tutoring me, and she brought them back to me since I was moving the next day.

After giving me my books, she walked towards the door, but my mother entered and found her in our house.

I knew I was in trouble since my mother didn't like Mrs. Sandoval.

"You! Where is my child?" Ms. Sandoval started shouting, asking my mother for answers.

"I don't know what you are talking about." My mother replied as she ran towards me and hugged me tightly from the side.

"Is that my girl? Is it her? Why did you steal her from me?" Ms. Sandoval asked; her voice was shaky yet powerful.

"I'm calling the police." She added and dialed 911.

My brain knew what was happening, but I still couldn't wrap my head around it. I was still confused.

*All this time, was I leaving with my kidnapper?*

Police sirens could be heard from miles away. My 'mother'

or rather, the kidnapper was still holding me tightly, so much so I couldn't breathe.

"Mom, let me go, you're hurting me," I tried to explain, but my pleas fell on deaf ears.

"Don't worry *mija*, the police will soon arrive." Mrs. Sandoval assured me.

Soon after, my kidnapper was arrested, and the court ruled that I was to stay with my actual mother, Maria Sandoval.

## THE TIME TRAVELER

In a tiny little town, there lived a little boy. His name was James. He lived with his Aunt called Marie, who took care of him. James missed his mother a lot, and he would often think about a story his mother told him as a small child.

'A long time ago in the far east, there was once a farmer who had a big farm. He kept animals of all kinds. But he loved his chickens most. Every day he would go to his farm and say these three little words, " Come forth thee." And when his animals heard his sound, they would start making all kinds of noises.

The older man would laugh and feed them. One day as he was digging up potatoes on his farm, he came across a shiny red object. It was the most beautiful jewelry he had ever seen. He couldn't stop staring at it.

But when he picked it up, a glowing red light filled the sky, and the bright light blinded him.

As he looked around, his farm had disappeared together with his house. He started running and screaming out, " My farm, my chickens, where are you?" but he was no longer on the farm. The small red jewelry was still glowing. He dropped it to the ground and wept. As he looked down, he noticed he had different clothes. " Where am I ?" He asked himself. He looked around and saw so many houses and trees. He decided to go to one of the houses and find out where he was.'

"What happened next?" Little James asked.

"It's time for you to sleep, that's what's next." Jame's mother told him.

"Pretty please, I want to know what happened next." Little James cried out.

"I'll let you know when I come back from work in the morning. I promise." His mother said and kissed him.

That was the last time he saw his mother's beautiful smile. He would cry himself to sleep at night, wishing his mother would come back. Aunt Marie would make him cookies and milk in the morning before he went to school and give him warm hugs and kisses. But James didn't want Aunt Marie to hug him; he wanted his mother.

"Aunt Marie, when is Mom coming back?" James

would ask every morning.

"Soon, my small boy. Now come along before you get late for school."

At school, James was brilliant, and his Science teacher, Mr. Mash, liked him very much. He would pick him to answer the most challenging questions in class, and James would answer them correctly.

But he could no longer concentrate in class as he would think about his mother and the story about the strange older man. James wondered where his mother had gone. Kids in school would bully him and make fun of him when the teacher would ask him a question, and he would get it wrong.

"James, are you okay?" Mr. Mash asked.

"Yes sir." James answered in a shy voice.

"I noticed you are not concentrating a lot in class. Do you need some extra help?"

James nodded.

"Okay then. The science fair is around the corner, I hope you are ready. You could win that scholarship and become a great scientist in the future. You are my best student and if you need help you can always come to me." Mr. Mash said while smiling.

"Thank you sir." James smiled back.

As James walked home that day, two boys from his school approached him. He knew them. They were Jill and Joe, the two bullies in school. He didn't like them one bit. And he knew they were here to bully him. Without thinking, James started running.

"Run little rat, we are going to catch you anyway." Joe shouted.

And the two boys began chasing James down the road. James was very fast too, and he was used to being bullied by them. So he ran through small alleys and threw random objects at them.

As he was about to escape them, he bumped into an older man, and they both fell. The older man wore as though he came out of the Victorian era. He also had a long white goatee. He didn't look like anyone James knew.

James was fascinated by the older man's looks, but he remembered his troubles.

"I'm so sorry old man."

As he looked behind, Jill and Joe had caught up with him. There was no place he could run to. He tried to help the older man up.

"You thought you could run away from us?" Jill sneered.

"It's time to teach you a lesson, you little punk." Joe said as he walked towards James and the older man.

"Stop right there young man." The older man spoke for the first time.

"And who do you think you are?" Joe asked.

After a long silence between both groups, the older man removed the old cloak covering him.

"I am a time Traveler," the old man said.

The two boys laughed.

"Get out of our way you crazy old man," said Jill.

And before the two boys could move, the older man revealed a shiny red object from his pocket that glowed so bright. The two boys got scared and ran away.

"That will teach them a lesson." The older man said and laughed.

James could not believe his eyes. It was the older man from the storybook. Could it be true? Was he the older man his mother had told him about?

"It can't be." James said to himself.

"Trust me they won't bother you again," the old man said while walking away.

"Who are you? Are you the old man from the tales? Where did you come from? Where is my mother?" James was now shouting in shock and fear.

"Come down little man. What fairy tales?" The older man asked.

James narrated the story to the older man. The man listened carefully and looked at James.

"That's not me. I'm sorry, kid, but I don't know your mother or the man with the farm.'

James was not happy to hear about this. The older man felt moved by the little boy.

"If it makes you feel better, I'll tell you where I came from and I do need a place to stay." The older man said while in deep thoughts.

"Well you can come with me, Aunt Marie has a spare room. And you can tell me all about it at home. It's getting late and she will be worried."

Little James walked home with the strange older man from the alley. Aunt Marie was waiting for him outside the house.

"Where have you been, I was worried sick that something bad happened to you," Aunt Marie cried.

"I'm okay Auntie. This old man helped me. Two boys from my school were chasing me. His name is.."

"Hello Ma'am, my name is Kazen the time Traveler."

" Nice to meet you Kazen the.."

"Time Traveler."

"Auntie, can he stay with us? He doesn't have anywhere to go." James pleaded.

"He can definitely join us. The more the merrier right?" Aunt Marie said.

"You are the best!" James hugged his Aunt.

They all got inside the house and had a wonderful meal together. Kazen told them about his amazing traveling stories and the worlds beyond. As James went to bed, he thought of his mother and the stories Kazen told him.

The following day as James was getting ready to go to school, Kazen told him something.

"I have been traveling all over the world looking for someone to take this jewelry from me so that I can now rest. And you are the only one who welcomed me to their home. So I leave this to you." Kazen handed the red ruby to James.

"Guard it with your life and don't lose it. It will help you find what you are looking for." He added.

And then Kazen disappeared into thin air.

A week passed, and James never saw the older man again. He carried the red ruby everywhere he went hoping Kazen would come back. The science fair came, and James was awarded the best student. Mr. Mash was so proud of himself and James too.

As James prepared to go to his new school, he found a note in his mother's room.

*You are the chosen one.*

*Kazen the Time Traveler.*

"James hurry up or you'll miss your flight," Aunt Marie called him.

On the plane, James felt the ruby glowing from his pocket. He closed his eyes and made a wish.

"I wish for a new start and to find my mother."

A blinding red glow filled the plane. And everything went dark. When James woke up, everything had changed.

## THE THREE R'S

It was a lovely evening in the kingdom of Tielles. Everyone was happy with life.

The prince arrived on this fateful day. He had grown into a fine young man, and it was time to find a beautiful and humble wife to settle down. The king arranged for a grand ball where the prince would choose his soon-to-be wife.

Every maiden was invited to the ball. Girls traveled far and wide to try their luck throughout the region, hoping they would turn into princesses during that enchanting night.

Well, everyone except a special girl known as Robyn.

Robyn was the most beautiful girl in the northern region—every man offered her a hand in marriage, but she declined. All she ever wanted was to travel the world.

"Are you going to the ball?" Robyn's father, Henry, asked.

"Why father? You know those things are not for me!" She explained.

"Sometimes you can find magic in places you never thought you would find it." Henry insisted.

"I understand but I'll find magic somewhere else." Robyn said.

"Where? At what time? Nothing lasts forever, don't wait for tomorrow Robyn." Henry says as he gives Robyn a peck on her forehead. "Goodnight, my princess." He adds as he leaves.

"I'm not a princess, I'm so much more." Robyn whispers.

The next day, the sun rose, casting golden rays through Robyn's window, waking her up for the long day.

Since girls from each region had come to town to try their luck—it was crowded, filled with sweet scents and pretty faces.

"If only my life was as simple as this!" Robyn said.

At the market, there was a colorful explosion. All the shops selling dresses were full. Every girl wanted to look their best on this special night.

On the other hand, Robyn bought groceries and

headed back home, but since the market was crowded, she bumped into a girl and dropped all her groceries.

"Hey! Watch where you're going!" The girl shrugged.

Robyn knelt to pick up her grocery and looked behind to see who she had bumped into. The girl looked identical to her! This was shocking to see. When the girl looked back, she realized the same thing, and the two walked towards each other.

"Why do you look like me?" They both asked at the same time.

This was a little *weird*.

The other girl held Robyn and led her to an allay,

"Why do we look alike?" She asked.

"I don't know but we have to find out." Robyn replied.

"I'm going to the ball tonight but we can find out why after. You can find me at this address. My name is Renee." She said,

"I'm Robyn, I'm pleased to meet you even though you owe me fresh groceries." Robyn said.

"I'm in a rush. Find me tomorrow to solve the mystery." Renee said as she ran towards the market.

"What about my groceries?" Robyn asked.

"Tomorrow!" Renee exclaimed as she disappeared among the people at the market.

As Robyn walked back home, she couldn't help but

notice another girl who looked like her as well! She was at a Tailor's shop.

Unlike her and Renee, this girl didn't look 'ordinary.' It seemed like she was from a wealthy family.

Robyn decided to approach her, hoping she'd agree to solve the mystery with her and Renee, but the butler mistook her for the rich girl when she arrived. After trying to explain she wasn't Reece—the rich girl, the butler wasn't having any of it, and so he carried her to the horse chariot, and they took off.

Once they arrived, she was shocked to see how extravagant the place was.

Reece's parents greeted her warmly, thinking she was their daughter.

She had to craft a plan to escape once she arrived at Reece's room.

While everyone was busy ushering in, the prince came to see his longtime friend, Reece, before the ball.

Robyn took that opportunity to escape after meeting him but little did she know the prince disliked get-togethers and preferred to sit by himself.

As she jumped off the fence, the prince caught her red-handed since he had escaped as well.

"Reece would never jump off a fence, who are you?" The prince asked.

"It's me. I just developed new hobbies while you were away," Robyn tried to explain.

The prince started laughing.

"That's a lie! Who are you and why do you look so much like Reece?" The prince insisted.

"If you let me go, perhaps, I'll tell you." Robyn said.

"Where are you in a hurry to go to?" The prince asks.

"I need to go home. The butler mistook me for Reece since we look alike. I bet she's stranded. Since you're her friend, you need to send someone to pick her up." Robyn advised.

"Alright! I'll do that and I'll only let you go, if you take me with you." The prince offered.

"Why do you want to go with me and where can I take a prince like you?" Robyn asked.

"It's just that you talk to me like a regular person. You don't feen over me like others do, I like that. You can take me anywhere you'd like." Said the prince.

"Do we really have to?" Robyn asked.

"Yes, we do." The prince replies.

The prince sent his butler to fetch Reece while he had a beautiful afternoon filled with friendship and laughter with Robyn.

"Don't you have a ball to go to?" Robyn asked.

"If I'm being honest, I prefer to meet someone and fall in love slowly until one day, you find yourself doing things you never thought you would, then you realize it's your love for that person that's making you do all those things."

The prince explained.

"I didn't know you were so…" Robyn said.

"Deep?" The prince interrupted.

"Yes, I thought you were shallow." Robyn commented.

"Well, I have to go. Thank you for the wonderful evening. I hope to see you at the ball." The Prince said.

"It's very unlikely, balls aren't my *thing*." Robyn insisted.

"So, what is your *thing*?" The prince asked.

"Adventure." Robyn replied.

"Well, I still hope to see you." The prince said.

The sun fell away and rested.

The sky was pitch black, the moon and stars shined brightly.

Robyn's encounter with the prince proved that people are not what they seem, but still, she had to solve the mystery of her life.

*Why did Reece and Renee look just like her!*

To find the answers to her questions, she decided to go to the ball to see the two girls.

Her dad was glad that she had changed her mind, but still, she didn't have a dress to wear!

Thankfully, Henry gave Robyn access to her mother's closet.

"Why does mom have so many expensive dresses? These are beautiful." Robyn asked.

"She was a famous tailor and made dresses for

Queens and Princesses. You can pick your favorite one." Henry replied.

Seeing her mother's dresses made Robyn feel connected to her mother once again.

Robyn's mother had died during childbirth, and she knew little about her.

She picked a red dress that had pearls that glistened like rubies.

"You look beautiful." Henry assured her.

Each girl was picked up by a horse chariot sent by the royal family. Her Chariot finally arrived, and she went to the palace accompanied by her father, Henry.

As she arrived, everyone gasped. She looked utterly beautiful.

Robyn looked for Reece and Renee until she found them. Since Reece wasn't aware she had lookalikes, she was extremely shocked, but she soon understood they had a mystery.

On the other hand, the prince danced with different maidens throughout the night but still hoped to see Robyn at the ball.

The three maidens decided to come clean in front of their parents to demand an explanation.

When they revealed they were identical to each other, their parents were shocked as well.

They didn't understand how they looked similar, but they agreed to summon the midwife who helped while their mothers gave birth to the three girls. The following day, they would find the answers to their questions

As Robyn was leaving the palace since everything she had come to do was accomplished, she met the prince outside the gate.

"Escaping, again?" The prince asked.

Robyn chuckled, and the two eloped to somewhere adventurous and fun.

The following day, the parents of the girls met the midwife.

The girls shortly joined their area of the meeting.

"Three women once gave birth to children but two of the women's children died during childbirth. The third woman gave birth to triplets and since she couldn't afford to bring them up due to poverty, she gave the two children away without the knowledge of the other two women." The midwife explained.

Despite all these events, there was no rift created. This brought the families together. The girls built a strong, unbreakable bond.

The prince eventually proposed to his dear friend, Robyn, and the two traveled the world together until it was time for the prince to become the king.

# LOST IN SPACE

In a gloomy town, the news of lost astronauts spread like wildfire.

The group had lost their way back home after disappearing into outer space.

"Did you hear about what happened?" Kai asks his robot, Kenny.

"It's terrible!" Kenny replies.

"Where could they have gone?" Kai asks.

"I can't tell unless we know what truly happened." Kenny says.

"By going to space and looking for clues?" Kai asks.

"Yes, Kai." Kenny replies.

Ever since birth, Kai's stars aligned, and ever so often, he dreamt of a life in space.

With every step he took around the sun, his curiosity expanded like the universe, and with the help of his robot, he was able to find answers to his questions.

Since Kai was fascinated by outer space and the solar and his magical Robot, Kenny allowed him to travel to the milky way once in a while.

One day, Kai would become an Astronaut and find his own space in orbit, but before that happens, his trips to outer space taught him more than what they taught at NASA.

On a special day, Kai's revealed to his best friends, Aiko and Lucas, that his robot was magical.

"We can go to Outer Space with the help of my magical robot, Kenny, to discover more about the missing astronauts," Kai suggested.

"Toy robots can't do anything out of the ordinary. Instead, we can meet at my place." Aiko disagreed.

"But—it's true and Kenny is not a toy, he's real." Kai insists.

"Okay! Then prove it!" Aiko says. "Lucas, you seem stressed!" Aiko adds while looking at Lucas.

"Surface tension!" Lucas replies.

Kai and Aiko burst out laughing.

"Would you look at that! Finally the two of you are doing the same thing without arguing!" Says Lucas.

"Haha! So funny Lucas. Come on, let's go to Kai's house to meet his 'magical robot'." Aiko says mockingly.

The trio walks up the hill to Kai's house.

"Kai, there's nothing unusual about your Robot!" Aiko says as she looks at Kenny, the robot.

"Nothing unusual? Well, there's nothing usual about me." Kenny says as he comes to life.

"What should I build for you, Kai?" Kenny asks.

Aiko and Lucas are shocked to see Kenny talking.

"Do you want to go to space to solve the mystery of the missing astronauts?" Kenny asks.

Aiko couldn't understand how the robot was talking, she stood still, gazing at the robot.

"Aiko, it seems like you are in Jupiter, earth to aiko?" Lucas says as he snaps his fingers in front of Aiko's eyes.

"Lucas! Stop it!" Aiko says as she pushes Lucas' hand away.

"So, you were right Kai! When can you build the Rocket?" Aiko asks Kenny.

"I am a magical robot, it will only take two seconds." Kenny replies, and immediately, a rocket appears.

"It's time to blast off!" Kenny adds on.

"Well, you don't have to tell me twice! I was ready yesterday!" Lucas says as he wears a Spacesuit and enters the rocket

Kai and Aiko burst out laughing.

The three kids and Kenny voyaged deep into space.

Space was an exciting place to be, there were so

many places to explore, but their main focus was to find out what happened to the missing astronauts.

"All of these discoveries are fun but I am a bit disappointed!" Lucas says.

"Why?" Kai asks.

"There are no cows in the milky way." Lucas replies.

The whole crew laughs while floating in space.

"Kenny, which planet did the astronauts disappear to?" Kai asks.

"Mars!"

"Alright! Mars, here we come!" Kai says

The crew hurtles the spaceship to Mars.

The planet was rocky, and red dust covered the whole planet.

"I don't like this planet, it's not as colorful as Earth." Aiko says.

As soon as Lucas went out of the Rocket, he came back breathing heavily.

"I bet Earth makes fun of these other planets for having no life!" Lucas says.

The group laughed hysterically.

"Yes, this planet doesn't have oxygen. It can't support a human's life." Kenny adds on.

"So where could the Astronauts have disappeared to!" Kai asked Kenny.

"It's hard to breathe without an oxygen tank on this planet. I don't think they survived. And if they did, there's something beautiful going on in the galaxy—something that's breathing out oxygen on this planet." Kenny explained.

"But what could be breathing out oxygen?" Kai asked.

"Special plants." Kenny said.

The group explored the planet, but they couldn't find clues leading to the astronauts' disappearance.

"Where should we go next?" Aiko asks.

"Back home! Earth is the only planet that supports life. Our mission is complete. The astronauts didn't survive," Kai says.

The crewmates fixed every latch in the Rocket, and just when they were about to take off, they saw the light shining from a distance.

"Guys look!" Kai said as he pointed towards the light.

"Don't get too excited, we need to wear our oxygen tanks and spacesuits and find out who or what that is." Kenny explained.

The group did as they were told and walked towards the light.

As they arrived, they were shocked to see one of the Astronauts.

"We got lost on this planet when we were exploring. But, the most important thing is, we found life on this planet." The Astronaut explained.

"Where are the rest?" Lucas asked.

"Back at our spot. We found plants that breathe out oxygen after breathing in this rare air." The astronaut explained.

Eventually, they all went back home using their rocket.

It was an adventure of a lifetime.

NASA recognized the group, and they were offered full scholarships.

The news of a group of kids and their robot saving the Astronauts stuck in space made headlines worldwide.

## WHEN THE SIREN CALLS

After the death of my grandfather, we had to go back to his hometown. His castle lay in the middle of a deep gloomy wood by an abandoned beach. Everything about the castle was unusual, and thinking about it gave me goosebumps. Creepy experiences kept happening around the house. It felt as though my grandfather's soul wasn't resting in peace—or it was just my imagination.

My mother explained that would be our new home because that's what grandfather would have wanted. At first, I was angry about the whole thing, but soon I realized that I could do nothing to change her mind and tried to adjust.

My little sister, Lory, was different. Instead of finding the castle scary, she thought it was fun and adventurous.

Every morning, I woke up early to take runs by the beach. Even though it wasn't as pretty as the beaches back in California, it still calmed me down and made me a little happy. It felt as though I had a piece of home with me.

At first, the morning runs were completely normal, but after a few weeks, I started noticing something peculiar.

On a cold morning, I woke up and went to the beach for my regular run. As I was tying my shoes to get ready to run, I couldn't help but notice someone had written, "HELP ME!" on the sand.

*Who could it be? Who needs my help? Or, perhaps it's nothing.*

"IT'S NOT NOTHING! HELP ME." Another writing said,

*How is this person reading my mind? Who could it be?*

These events creeped me out, and I immediately retreated. Instead of going for my regular run, I went back home.

Eventually, I convinced myself it was all in my head. Afterward, Lory and I went to school.

The day was uneventful and boring. The kids at school were mean and nicknamed us "the creepy Shelleys" because Shelley was our second name, passed on to us by our grandfather.

As we walked home, I saw another message scribbled on a tree.

"HELP ME TORY!"

*How did the person who wrote it know my name? What kind of help were they looking for?*

"SAVE ME!" another message was scribbled on another tree.

"Perhaps someone is playing a cruel trick on me. It could be someone from school since they were not very receptive ever since we moved." I thought.

The evening went by pretty quickly, and finally, it was night. We all went downstairs to eat dinner.

"Mother, do you think this town is *weird*?" I asked.

"It's a bit unusual but I had the best moments in this house while growing up. Why? What's the matter?" She replied.

"Can't we go back home? Please?" I asked politely, hoping to convince her.

"Tory! Again with that? If your little sister was able to adjust, why can't you give this town a chance?" She said as she held my hand.

I immediately freed my hand from her touch and went upstairs. I had to solve my problems on my own.

I documented each message I got and went to sleep.

The next day, I woke up early in the morning for my run. As I arrived at the beach, I didn't find a message this time, so I went on with my day.

Weeks passed by, and still, I didn't get any messages. I realized that high chances are it was just a prank from the kids at school.

On a fateful day, as I woke up for my morning run. I found a letter from an anonymous person in the drawer beside my bed.

"Dear Bean,

I need your help. You need to figure out where I am because I can't tell — I'm stuck."

"Bean? My grandfather used to call me that! Could he be the one sending these messages? Who's helping him send them? If I found out who that person is, they might lead me to him. Or, could this be a tasteless prank made by the kids at school." I started thinking out loud.

"But grandfather is *dead*. But we also didn't bury him. His body was lost at sea." These thoughts ran through my mind.

"How is he sending these letters? The person sending them can definitely read my mind. Is he being held by a mythical creature? A mermaid maybe?" More thoughts popped up in my mind.

I had to catch a breath, and so I went downstairs to drink water.

It all felt like a lie! A fantasy because Grandfather had died, and none of this was possible.

Since Lory was more receptive to peculiar events, I went to her room and told her what was happening.

To my shock and surprise, she had also been receiving such messages, and they were all from Grandpa.

We promised to find and bring him back home safely.

Since it was a school day, we prepared and went to class. The day moved pretty quickly. Lory and I went to class and came back home to plan the rescue operation.

"We don't even know what happened to grandpa. Mother hides it. How can we solve this if we don't have the most basic information?" Lory said.

Even though Lory was the youngest, she was smart, and everything she said made sense.

We went to Grandpa's room to find clues leading us to his disappearance. After searching for countless hours, the only thing we found was a letter. The hand-writing was pretty, and so perhaps a woman wrote it.

"Ever since I met you, I knew you were the one. Meet me at the caves tonight."

"What if this woman kidnapped Grandpa and she's the one playing this horrible trick by sending us letters and random messages? We need to go to the Caves to see if we can find Grandpa." Lory suggested.

"I don't know about this, it all feels fishy but if we can find grandpa, that will be great. Since tomorrow is the weekend, we can go there early in the morning." I added.

The two of us agreed.

That night, I couldn't sleep. Thousands of thoughts ran through my mind.

Eventually, morning arrived, and we went to the caves, but nobody was there.

As soon as we were about to leave, we heard someone coughing—it was Grandpa!

We found a secret door with stairs leading to the ground floor of the cave, and as we arrived, Grandpa was being held there.

"Grandpa! Are you alright!." We both said consecutively as we rushed to untie him from the chair.

"Oh! My girls! I didn't think I would be found." He said.

Lory immediately called mother and told her what was happening, but as we tried to leave, a beautiful woman walked in and tried to stop us.

"Where do you think you are going?" She said,

"If you know what's best for you, let us leave." My Grandfather said.

"And why would I do that?" The woman said.

Soon after, the woman let out a scream, and the caves started tumbling down.

She was a siren! A wicked mermaid and my grandfather had fallen victim to her. He thought she was a regular woman.

We tried to find a place to elope safely, but we were trapped in ruins. I tried to use my phone, but it crashed while we were escaping to a safe spot.

Eventually, we heard sirens. The police cars were approaching. We were rescued, and our mother gave us a warm embrace. She was happy to see her father once again.

The siren disappeared without a trace, but Lory and I promised to track and take her down sooner or later.

## THE BOY WHO CRIED "ALIEN"!

"I saw an Alien Spaceship last night!" Shawn explains to his friends as they walk home from school.

"That's not true! Aliens don't exist." Mai disagrees.

"Aliens exist! I saw the Rocket voyage deep into space after dropping an alien on Earth!" Shawn insists.

"Wait! If aliens exist does that mean that Cows can go to space too?" Peter asks goofily.

"To do what?" Shawn replies.

"To see the Milky Way!" Peter says as he starts laughing.

"Hold on! Peter, do you believe him? Well, I don't! First, you'll have to prove it's true. The only planet that supports life is Earth." Mai says.

"Well, don't get astrophysical with me! I'm just trying to make the two of you laugh!" Peter replies.

"If you don't believe me, you can come to my place tonight and we'll see the Alien's spacecraft!" Shawn says.

The sun fell away and rested for a while.

The trio waited by Shawn's window, looking through a magical Telescope to see an alien spacecraft in the sky.

The moon was full, and the stars were bright, but there was no sign of an alien spaceship—at least when Mai and Peter looked through the Telescope.

But when Shawn looked, there was an Alien spaceship in the Sky.

"There it is!" Shawn said as he gave Mai the Telescope."

"I can't see anything!" She says. "You're lying again Shawn!"

"I promise I'm not!" Shawn insists.

"Arrrghhh!" Mai shrugged off and left.

Peter bid Shawn goodbye, and the duo was driven home by Shawn's mom.

After some time, Shawn fell asleep.

"Kkrrrr! Krrr!" The alarm buzzed.

It was time for school!

Shawn felt uneasy, he didn't understand why he could see the Aliens, but his friends couldn't.

When he arrived at school, Mai avoided him, but Peter walked to class for the science lesson with him.

Mrs. Sandoval enters the classroom, and everyone stands up to greet her.

The lesson ended quickly, and Shawn approached Peter and Mai.

"I'll prove I saw an alien. Can you come to my house tonight?" Shawn asked.

"Again with that? I thought we were past this, Shawn." Mai exclaimed.

"Well, I'm not and I want to prove what I said is true." Shawn replies.

"Alright! We'll be there." Peter says.

"Peter!" Mai exclaims.

"What?" Peter asks.

"I don't want to do this again! You'll see, he's definitely lying!" Mai says.

"Alright! We'll have to catch him red-handed then." Peter says.

"But we already did! Remember?" Mai says.

"Just give him another chance Mai!" Peter says.

"Alright!" Mai agrees.

On that fateful evening, the duo headed over to Shawn's house for a sleepover.

Shawn's mother gave Mai and Peter a warm welcome.

In Shawn's bedroom, Mai and Peter looked through the Telescope to see if an Alien's spaceship would land on Earth, but they didn't see anything!

When Shawn took the Telescope to watch the stars, he saw an Alien spaceship, and the pilot waved at him.

"I saw it! Another Spaceship! The pilot just waved at me!

"Let me see!" Mai said as she snatched the Telescope from Shawn to see if his claims were true.

"There's no Spacecraft in the Sky!" Mai says.

"But..but.." Shawn stummers.

"Peter? Now, do you understand why I didn't want to come? He's lying to us...again!" Mai explains.

When Shawn looked through the Telescope once again, he could see more spaceships disappearing through Space.

"But guys, I'm telling you the truth! I can actually see Aliens." Shawn says.

"Stop it!! You are..."

Before Mai could complete the sentence, something extraordinary happened. A portal suddenly appeared!

"Now, can you see? I was telling you the truth." Shawn says.

"Well, it's just a portal, it doesn't prove whether you saw aliens or not!" Mai responds.

"Stop being so hard on him, he clearly wasn't lying." Peter adds on.

"We can go through the portal to discover what's on the other side. It could be an alien, a new universe or a new planet!" Shawn suggests.

"That's way too dangerous!" Mai warns Shawn.

"Are you chickening out? I thought you wanted to see aliens?" Shawn asks.

"Well, we could go but only for a few minutes!" Mai says.

"Alright! That's more like it!" Peter says excitedly.

The trio enters the portal and completely vanishes from the face of the earth!

The portal took them to an unknown planet.

As they arrived, they were amazed and terrified at the same time!

The creatures who lived on this peculiar planet looked different.

The planet was covered in sand, and there was no sun. Instead, they got their light from the millions of stars shining from the pitch-black sky.

The creatures were shocked to see the trio.

"Aliens! They exist!" One creature exclaimed in both fear and excitement.

"Why are they calling us aliens, they are the aliens —not us!" Mai whispers.

Shawn and Peter didn't have an answer to the question, so they remained silent.

"Guys! We have to go home." Mai whispers, but the boys ignore her. Their eyes were glued on the creatures of this bizarre planet where the sun didn't shine.

These creatures were different from the aliens Shawn had previously seen.

The aliens weren't hostile. In fact, they welcomed the trio to their weird planet.

Shawn was still unsatisfied. He needed to know who the other aliens on earth were because these aliens had never left their homes and were shocked to see the trio.

"Guys, these aren't the aliens that I saw back home." Shawn explained.

"What? Then, why did the portal appear in your room?" Peter asked.

"I don't understand it either. Maybe there's a glitch in the galaxy." Shawn said. "Since you believe me, we can go home and solve the mystery. There's something wrong." Shawn added on.

The trio went back where the portal was and traveled back home.

After school, the next day, they met at Shawn's place and camped outside, hoping to find out what the problem was.

Shawn took his telescope and started observing the sky.

Eventually, Shawn could see the aliens landing on earth.

"They are at the beach. We have to go!" Shawn said.

"What? Why would they land at the beach?" Peter asked.

"It's the perfect place, humans can't breathe under-

water. They could be building their base underwater."
Shawn explained.

The trio took their bicycles and rode to the beach at night.

As they arrived, they saw a UFO plunging in the water.

As they approached it, an alien walked towards them.

"We are not here to hurt anyone. Our home was destroyed by the war," The alien said.

"What war?" Shawn asked.

"The alien planets are experiencing wars. The only peaceful planets are Red and Earth." He explained.

Eventually, the trio agreed to help the aliens and went to NASA for help.

The war of the planets was eventually settled.

The aliens were fighting for the light of the sun since their planets were pushed away from the sun.

Since some planets didn't have the sun, NASA gave them equipment to reflect the sun's light.

# THE MUMMY

Once upon a time, there lived an ancient Egyptian god who ruled vast lands. He was known as the god of war. He would go to other kingdoms and take their lands and treasures.

The people who remained became his servants and slaves. The more he took other possessions and treasures from other gods, the more he created enemies. No one wanted to be ruled by him.

So other gods came together and decided to destroy him. This was only possible by removing his heart from his chest, made from a beautiful sapphire stone.

One day, as the Egyptian god was making merry with his close friends, a servant poured something in his drink. This made him feel drowsy, and he was enchanted into a deep sleep.

A loud horn was blown to signal the other gods.

And as they plucked his heart out of his chest, his lovely wife was watching from afar. She swore to avenge his death and quickly ran away into hiding.

The ruler was mummified and buried with all his things as it was the custom of the Egyptians. Till this date, no one knows where the queen went. But it is said, she comes in the form of a beautiful shadow, and you should beware if she offers blue crystals to you."

Susan loved reading this storybook every time she went to the library at school. Her friends had nick-named her Cleopatra because she was fascinated by ancient Egypt. She never stopped talking about the book.

"Susan, one of these days we shall mummify you instead," her friend, Ben, told her.

"You cannot mummify the goddess, she will turn you into stone before you get the chance," Susan said while laughing.

"I guess we'll have to tie her eyes then." Ben said while putting his books in his bag.

Susan and Ben had been childhood friends before they could start walking. They lived across from each other, went to the same school, were in the same class, and their parents were best friends too. Therefore, they did everything together. Sleepovers were often done in Susan's home.

As they walked out of the library, they spotted a

new girl in school. She had blue eyes and the longest hair Susan had ever seen. She was gorgeous too.

"I see we have another Egyptian Queen in school," Ben teased Susan.

"Oh please! There can only be one Queen," Susan said. But deep down, she knew the girl would steal the show. The new girl turned and looked at them and waved. They waved back.

As they walked home, Susan could not stop thinking about the new girl.

"Someone is awfully quiet. Is everything okay Suzie?" Ben asked while adjusting his glasses.

"Yeah, I was just thinking about the upcoming trip to the museum. We can finally get to see the famous Egyptian gods. Do you know they have an exact replica of the heart of the Egyptian god?" Susan asked.

"How would I not know when you keep telling me every time," Ben said.

"Oh! I really do talk about it a lot." Susan agreed.

"Finally, you admit it." Ben added on.

"Well, the last one to get to the house is a mummy."

Before Ben could say anything, Susan had already started running. They both laughed as they raced to get home.

The next day, as they got to class, Susan found the new girl sitting on her chair, talking to her friend Alexis.

"Umm…excuse me, that's my seat." Susan explained.

The girl looked at her with her enchanting blue eyes and smiled at Susan.

"I'm sorry for taking your position. My name is Estrella. But my friends call me Ela." The new girl said.

"Okay Ela, can I have my seat back?" Susan asked.

"Sure." Estrella agreed.

Ela rose and whispered to Susan. "I can't wait for tomorrow, Egyptian Queen."

Susan felt uneasy.

She did not like Ela at all.

*And what did Ela mean by that?*

She could not stop thinking about tomorrow. After class, she decided to tell Ben what had happened.

During lunch hour, she could not find Ben. She decided to look for him at their chill spot. He was not there. That was very odd. As she was about to give up searching for him, she felt a tap on her shoulder. It was Ben.

"I have been looking everywhere……."

"Suzie this Ela, my new friend." Ben said while smiling.

"Your new friend?" Susan was surprised to see Ela.

"Yes, Ben and I met in the hallway after class. He is really a good friend," Ela explained.

"Ben, can I talk to you for a minute?" Susan could

not believe what was happening. She pulled Ben aside and told him what she thought about Ela.

"I don't think she's a bad person. She's actually sweet. Maybe if you get to know her, you'll change your mind," Ben said while adjusting his glasses.

"You just met her! I'm telling you, I don't feel safe around her. She looks like the evil queen from the book," Susan whispered.

"Hey guys, I can hear you from here. I know Suzie, you don't trust me. But I'll offer you a truce gift," Ela said while searching for something in her bag. She removed three blue crystals from her bag.

"One for everyone."

"I knew it. You are the evil queen from the book." Susan gasped.

"It's just a mythical story, Suzie. Stop it." Ben commented.

Her friend's words hurt Susan. She couldn't understand why Ben could not believe her.

The next day, everyone showed up for the trip to the museum. Susan and Ben did not sit together on the bus.

This was the first time they didn't do everything together. Ben sat next to Ela, his new friend. Susan missed Ben, but she wanted to prove him wrong.

"He is going to apologize for not believing me. You do believe me Alexis, right?" Susan asked.

"Yeah, Ben just has a crush on her. That's why he can't see it yet," Alexis said.

As the bus got near their destination, Susan made a plan. She would not lose sight of Ela to know what the 'evil queen' was up to.

Their History teacher grouped them into two teams. Ela was in the same group with Susan, while Ben ended up with Alexis. As both teams toured the museum, Susan kept a close eye on Ela, but she didn't do anything suspicious.

Maybe Susan had judged her wrongly. She decided to apologize to Ela after the trip was over. Susan just wanted the day to end.

As they were about to get on the bus, one of the guards approached their History teacher and told everyone to get inside the museum. An artifact had been stolen. Susan was sure it wasn't Ela. Who could it be? What had been stolen?

"Everyone gets in line, someone amongst us has taken a valuable item in the museum. It is a small sapphire stone. Save our time by coming forward or we shall be forced to call the police." The history teacher bellowed to frighten the group of kids.

No one moved or came forward.

"Alright, you leave me no choice. Frisk them," the teacher said to the guards.

"Wait," Alexis spoke up. "I know who has it."

She raised her hand and pointed to Ela. Everyone

started murmuring, looking at the new girl. Susan stepped forward to defend Ela, but Ben held her hand.

" I believe you." He said and smiled at her.

The guards went and got hold of Ela.

"Unhand me you mortals. I am the queen of Egypt. I shall avenge my husband. I summon thee," Ela commanded. But nothing happened. The stone was a piece of fake ruby jewelry.

"Okay enough drama Estrella. Return the ruby and I'm calling your parents." The history teacher said.

Susan was itching to know what had happened and how the ruby had been stolen.

"I had missed you best friend, now tell me everything," Susan said while hugging Ben.

"Well first of all, I'm sorry I said those hurtful things to you. Please forgive me." Ben said while adjusting his glasses.

Alexis came from behind and hugged them.

"That was awesome, we should do more Museum trips Ben," Alexis said while laughing.

They all laughed and walked towards the bus together.

"You know if Ela wasn't such a bad person, she would be another mini- Suzie. She couldn't stop talking about the Egyptian god," Ben said.

"There can only be one Egyptian Queen," Susan said, and they all laughed.

# LOST IN HISTORY

It was a winter wonderland in Kingsland. The snow covered the whole land in a thick white blanket. It was cold and felt as if the air was made of broken glass. A shy boy, Martin, was walking from school and headed to the train station.

On his way home, he loved to listen to music and ignore the passersby since it gave him a sense of peace —it made him feel as though he was the only person on earth.

On this typical day, nothing out of the ordinary occurred! Everything seemed fine, but that wasn't the case. Destiny had different plans for Martin on that fateful snowy day. As he got on the train, he stumbled upon the door and fell underneath the train tracks.

Since he was small and the train had a few passengers, he was the last to enter so no one noticed. He tried calling out for help, but no one answered his pleas! He knew that was his last day, so he started holding on to his necklace, gifted by his late mother. Martin felt terrible for his father—he had lost his wife in an unexplainable way, and now he'd lose Martin too!

Immediately the train's engine started grinding and was almost moving, Martin closed his eyes, and he vanished into thin air!

As he opened his eyes, he found himself in another city! In utter disbelief, he stood up and walked around the town trying to find his way back home but instead, he realized he was in the 1900s after reading the newspaper.

Martin was in shock; he didn't understand how he got into this era! The last thing he could remember was that he was beneath the train tracks, and he started holding his mother's necklace tightly!

*Could the necklace have brought him to the 1900s, or was it just a glitch in time!*

Thoughts ran through his mind, but he still couldn't find an answer to this peculiar event.

Since it was getting darker and the sun had just set, he decided to find shelter to escape the darkness and cold.

As he was walking on the streets, he saw someone he had studied in his science books! It was Albert Einstein!

Martin dashed to him and explained what was

happening, but Albert didn't believe him. He was a man of science, and magical necklaces didn't have any facts backing them up.

Martin didn't give up, and he explained about all his discoveries. This shocked Mr. Einstein.

"How did you know about how gravity works?" Mr. Einstein asked. He was eager to know how the little boy, Martin, could read his thoughts!

"Like I said, I'm from the future!" Martin replied.

"That's a lie! Or, perhaps time travel has been invented in the future?" Mr. Einstein asked.

"No! Not yet! I need you to help me find my way back home." Martin insisted.

"Listen, Kid, I have a lot on my plate and I can't deal with this now!" Mr. Einstein replied.

"But—I thought you wanted to be revolutionary, If you help me find my way back home! I'll tell them all about you in the future." Martin said.

"Little boy! Stop playing so much, I understand you are very creative and your imagination is very colorful and detailed but go home to your mother, I have some things I have to do!" Mr. Einstein explained.

"You don't understand." Martin went on until he realized that he was not going anywhere with Mr. Einstein, so he decided to find help somewhere.

He needed to know how he was able to time travel to the 1900s and if the necklace was responsible for time traveling or if it was a feeling he produced as he was feeling anxious under the train tracks.

Just as he was walking in the streets during the night, he met some weird-looking guys who tried to harm him, but he started running. He held onto his necklace, and he vanished in the 1980s. Martin couldn't wrap his head around what was happening, but one thing for sure was that it was all because of his mother's necklace!

While in the 1980s, he stumbled upon Micheal Jackson as he was heading to perform at a concert, and he chose to enjoy it!

At first, he had forgotten his worries, but he was reminded that he had to go home later on! His father must have been worried sick about his whereabouts!

As he was walking downtown, he was impressed by how colorful and lively the 80s seemed! The sun was shining and everyone just wanted to have fun and live life. So far, this was one of his favorite times in history.

Since he wanted the necklace to take him back to 2021, he went to a corner in the street, hoping no one would see him and held the chain tightly and whispered, "Take me back to 2021." He hoped that the necklace would listen to him, but that didn't happen! He didn't move an inch from where he was!

Suddenly, some kids spotted him, and they went to see why he was talking to a necklace.

"Look, he's talking to his necklace! He must be

crazy," one kid said. "No! He's not crazy just dumb!" Another one said, and they all started laughing at Martin hysterically.

At this moment, Martin knew that he couldn't ask these kids for help because they were rude and bullied him!

Instead, he walked away without saying a word to them, but they started following him, hurling insults. Since Martin was an intelligent young boy, he decided to run and escape not out of fear but because the kids could make things more difficult for him when all he was trying to do was get back home.

As he started running, the other children chased after him, and so he began holding his necklace firmly, and soon after, he disappeared.

Immediately after, he found himself in the Mesozoic era, and several Brontosaurus dinosaurs were being chased by T-rex, so he had to find a way to escape!

All that could ring in his mind was how to go back home! It was a complete mystery to him!

As they were approaching a steep area, he tried to fit himself in a small path that he didn't know where it was heading, and he successfully escaped the race to safety.

The era was beautiful due to its vegetation, but he still wanted to go home to his dad. Martin was getting frustrated as time went by because he didn't know what to do.

He tried to enjoy the adventure, but he was getting worried!

*What if he was lost and would never find a way back home!*

His thoughts tormented his little mind. He was hungry and needed water to drink, and so he went by the river. He was surprised to see how clear the water was, unlike the rivers from home that didn't have clean water.

As he was walking by the forest, he saw something that was sparkling in the trees. As he climbed up to get it, it was the other half of the necklace.

He attached the two pieces and immediately asked the necklace to take him back home.

After a few seconds, he was back at the train station, but he was outside the train, unlike the last time.

It's like nothing stopped when he was gone. In fact, time rewinded so that the accident wouldn't repeat itself, and Martin kept that in mind and carefully walked on the train without concentration on the music on his headphones.

Eventually, he arrived back home and hugged his father.

Martin's dad was shocked because he was never really affectionate even though he was a good kid.

That night, Martin couldn't sleep. He stayed up all night wondering about how his magical necklace allowed him to go back in the past!

*Can it also take me to the future? Or, Can I go back to meet my mom when she was just a girl! Even if she's lost now, I can still see her.*

Thoughts filled his mind, and he was getting more confident about time traveling!

The following day, after school, Martin went back in time to meet his mother.

His mother was a beautiful young woman, and she welcomed him warmly despite knowing he was her son from the future!

The two spent the day together, and Martin disclosed what had happened to him. His mother started explaining that she went on a time-traveling adventure a few days after he was born to clear her mind, but she got stuck in the year she was currently in.

They couldn't imagine that they would finally go back home together. Her son had come to rescue her. She was filled with happiness, and the two left and went back home.

As they arrived, Martin's father was shocked, but they all explained what had happened, and he decided to embrace his family. The three lived happily ever after and frequently traveled through time as a family.

# HEART OF A GIANT

Chase Brown was loved by his classmates. He had built a reputation for being a fun and adventurous person, making his peers love hanging out with him. There was also something unique about him, and his smile illuminated whatever room he entered.

Each day, he woke up excited and ready to go to school but on a sad day, his mother informed him that they were soon going to move to another town to live with the rest of their family.

"We'll be much happier and have support from our whole family," his mother assured.

"But—mother! I already have friends and moving to a new town in the middle of the term is not such a good idea," Chase replied.

"I understand but since your father passed away, I need more support," his mother tried to explain.

Chase didn't like to talk about his father—especially since his death was sudden and unexplainable.

"Alright mother! I accept," Chase agreed to make his mother feel better because she must've been dealing with the loss as well, and if she needed more support, it was alright.

"Thank you Chase! Your person will shine across no matter where you are! You are a special boy." His mother added.

"So, when are we leaving?" Chase asked.

"This Saturday! You have until tomorrow to bid your friends Goodbye!" Chase's mother said.

Chase resigned to his bed, and despite telling his mom he understood, he was still saddened that they would leave the town soon.

The next day, he visited his friends and bid them goodbye. They were all sad to hear the news, but due to his bubbly personality—he was bound to find beautiful adventures wherever he went, and that's what calmed him down.

As he arrived back home, he packed all his essentials. This part was somewhat complicated because Chase was the most well-put-together yet messiest person ever!

"Honey, let me help you with that," his mother said as she folded his clothes and packed them in his suitcase.

Chase sat on the bed and looked at his mother,

"Mother, my friends told me that the town we are moving to is a bit eerie." He said.

"Eerie? Hmm! I don't know about you but the Chase I know would look at that as an adventure," his mother said as she folded the last shirt, packed it in the suitcase, and closed it.

Chase didn't reply. The room was filled with silence.

"Oh, come on! Don't tell me you are scared?" His mother added.

"No! I'm just a bit hesitant when it comes to changes." Chase replied.

"I understand but this is for our overall well-being," his mother says as she sits beside him on the bed and kisses his forehead.

The Sun fell away and rested for some time, and Chase went to sleep. He was woken up the following day by his mother, and the two left for the airport.

After a few hours, their plane finally landed at Creepsdale. The town was silent, and everyone minded their own business. Unlike their previous village, Creepsdale wasn't colorful, and everyone wore dull colors.

The sky wasn't blue either and the Sun didn't grace the town with its golden hues. Everything was so different, but this didn't discourage Chase. Instead, he promised himself that he would try to find something worthwhile and that he would make friends at school.

Eventually, their relatives arrived to pick Chase and his mother from the airport. They arrived at a large castle in the middle of a gloomy forest. The castle looked as though it was built in the Victorian era.

"Welcome home!" Aunt Claude exclaimed.

The rest of their relatives were a bit kooky and gloomy, but Aunt Claude was filled with joy and had a bubbly personality similar to Chase's attitude.

The two got along, and during the first few days, they went on adventures together. So far, Chase had already adapted and loved living in Creepsdale until something peculiar occurred on a fateful morning.

As Chase took his horseback to the stables after a morning horse ride, he found giant footsteps inclined on the ground!

This was extremely shocking, especially since giants were extinct.

*What creature could have walked on their compound? Also, the fact that they lived in an area surrounded by a forest made it seem more real that there could be a large creature walking around!*

At the Market and school, he started hearing whispers from the townspeople about missing men who went hunting in the forest and never returned home!

*Could there be a dangerous creature living close?*

All this was hard to fathom, and so he dashed back home to ask his aunt.

"Well, I have heard about giants walking around this town but they were chased off!" His aunt replied.

"Where to?" Chase asked.

"It isn't known! The only person who can answer the question is your father." His aunt added.

"My father? What does he have to do with this?" Chase was eager to know, and so he asked.

"You aren't aware?" His aunt asked.

"Aware of what?" Chase replies.

"If you don't know yet, you'll have to wait to ask your mother!" She replied as she walked away.

Chase tried to call her, but she ignored him and walked further away.

Later on, he went to his room to rest and waited for his mother to come back, hoping he'd get an explanation.

*What did his father have to do with the Giants! Was what he saw the footprints of a giant?*

He expected the new town to be full of adventures, but this was a bit too much!

As soon as his mother arrived, he rushed to her room and asked, "Mother! Are there giants surrounding us and what does that have to do with dad?"

His mother remained quiet for a while and broke off the silence with a sigh.

"Mother, what is it?" Chase asked and patiently waited for an answer.

"Your father was one of the guardians of Creepsdale, there are giants but they only come when the key to their world is misplaced," she explained.

Chase was utterly shocked! He didn't quite understand why no one ever explained this before, but some of him was glad because he would eventually solve the problem.

"So, where are the keys? And how can I find the giants?" Chase asked.

"No one knows! Your father died trying to protect them! The giants are unexplainable creatures, it's hard to know where to find them." She went on.

"So dad died all because of this and you didn't tell me! Is that why we had to come back?" Chase asked.

"Yes, I'm also a guardian and I'm helping other guardians to find the keys but it has proven to be impossible and the giants keep harming the townspeople," she said.

"I just wish you told me about this!" Chase said.

"I know my son but all this is very dangerous and I was trying to protect you," she replied.

Chase was an understanding kid, so he forgave his mother but still swore to find the key.

That night, he couldn't sleep an inch! He kept tossing and turning in his bed because he was trying to figure out a plan that would eventually turn out to be successful.

Soon after, without realizing it, he fell into a deep

slumber, and as he woke up the next day, he went to the stables to find clues, but all he could see was a large piece of bread and crumbs leading to the forest.

*Should I follow the crumbs? What if I get lost? I'm new to this town!*

Regardless of his fears, he trusted his gut and decided to follow the breadcrumbs trail.

He walked until he arrived at the heart of the forest, but there was nothing to see!

He didn't give up, though, and he kept looking; he hoped he would find his way back home during that evening. After walking for a longer distance, he arrived at a place with monumental staircases that didn't seem as though they were for humans but giants!

He decided to climb to find clues despite knowing how violent giants could be. The staircases were large, and just climbing them felt like climbing a hill, but he was determined to help the townspeople and honor his father, a guardian, by finding the keys.

As he arrived at the top, the Giants were playing chess, and so he gathered courage and approached them, but he was shocked at the events that happened after.

*The giants were scared of him! Why? He was the size of a mouse compared to them! So, were the rumors true? Did the giants hurt people?*

After convincing the giants that he didn't mean any harm, they let him sit with them.

Chase explained what was happening, and the giants assured him that they were not the ones causing harm, and in fact, the humans were the ones who were hostile to them.

They explained that his father used to guide them from harm, but after his death, a lot of giants were dying.

"So where can I find the key to send you to safety?" Chase asked.

"We are already safe here. This is our home too! We don't understand why humans refuse to share it with us!" The leader of the giants replied.

At this point, Chase realized that he had to make a bigger decision than his father had ever made! He had to change the townspeople's way of thinking, making them receptive to the giants, living happily ever after, but that wasn't an easy goal to achieve, especially since Giants were portrayed as villains. Still, he had to find a way to stop the tension permanently.

One of the giants took him back home, and Chase explained to his mother what had happened. At first, she was hesitant, but she gave in and agreed to help her later on. They eventually changed their relatives' minds but it was time to change the villagers' minds.

On a fateful day, as Chase was walking in the forest with one of the giants, a poacher tried to hurt the giant. He hid on top of the tree and carefully waited to get a perfect shot, and just as he was about to release the arrow, he tripped and fell off the tree, but the giant held him, and he didn't fall on the rocks on the ground.

Instead of being violent like what other villagers had said, the giants carefully placed the man down, and that was when the man apologized and promised to spread the word that giants weren't villains but could be their heroes.

The word spread across the town, and slowly by slowly, people started to accept the giants. Eventually, humans and giants in Creepsdale lived in complete harmony, and Chase finally found exactly what he was looking for—friends with whom he'd have forest adventures.

# INTO THE FOREST

The sun sank towards the horizon, welcoming a harsh wind that blew the trees, forcing them to bend. The stars lit up the sky in the velvety darkness. Frost grew over the windows of a tiny house on the tip of the Mountain.

Maurice dashed to his attic and gathered everything he needed for his next adventure; he loved to visit eerie places with his friends, and together, they'd make weird yet unforgettable memories.

During the next day, they would visit the enchanted forest which lay between the shadow valley. The forest's reputation wasn't entirely good. However, the group was obsessed with exploring peculiar places, and so they decided they would go for the adventure and eventually tick off the forest from their to-do list. The villagers had warned that it was dangerous, but it was worth a try to the group.

After touring a particular place, the group always carried souvenirs to prove to their other friends how tough they were because they eventually made it to the scariest places in the town.

After packing his bag by adding everything he needed during the trip, Maurice resigned to bed, hoping the big day would approach as fast as possible. Despite trying to sleep countless times, Maurice was too excited yet a bit scared, which was expected because it was a new scary adventure, and he didn't know what to expect in the forest.

*Will I be able to see jaguars! Or perhaps lions or a kooky creature that no one has ever had before.*

These thoughts ran across his mind, but he had to wait to experience and see everything in person.

After a few hours, the day dawned clear, and the sun cast a faint yellow light through Maurice's window. He woke up and prepared a strong breakfast with the help of his mother to make sure

He was full throughout the journey to the Forest.

Immediately after he finished his breakfast, he heard a loud knock on the door. His friends Jack and Ohana had just arrived, Robin was as late as usual, so they decided to wait for him.

The trio decided to go to Maurice's room, where

they could check their bags to see if they had gathered everything they needed for their trip to the woods.

After double-checking and adding anything they left out, they went out and finally met Finnick in the alley.

They all took their bikes and rode off to the forest. During the journey, Jack tried to crack jokes to lessen the tension, but it was clear, the village people were right. As the kids entered the spooky forest, it felt as though the trees were looking at them, but each time they stared back—everything seemed normal.

The wind blew strongly, and Maurice accidentally bit his lips due to anxiety. He was the group's leader, but he felt as though something wasn't right. To make it worse, the fishy taste of blood in his mouth made him nauseous.

The kids would agree the enchanted forest was a hair-raising place. Regardless, that didn't stop them from going further into the woods.

Just as they were about to cross an old bridge, the winds blew hissing, "Welcome! Welcome!"

"Do you hear that?" Ohana whispered.

"What?" The rest of the kids asked.

"It's like the wind is talking directly to us!" Ohana replied.

"It's all in your head! Let's cross the bridge." Finnick replied.

As they started crossing, the hisses grew stronger and clearer than ever before.

"Finnick, can you hear the wind?" Ohana asked again.

"Maybe we should go back home." Finnick replied.

Jack giggled and replied, "No way! We have already made it so far! We need to keep going.

Eventually, they crossed the bridge, and the whispers disappeared.

This gave them the confidence to keep going, hoping they'd discover something more unique than what anyone in the village had seen.

As they arrived at a swamp, they saw a child jump in the soggy water and swim to the other side. They tried to call on him to warn him, but he had already made it to the other side.

"Impossible! How can one swim in a swamp!" Finnick said, "We need to head back home! This adventure isn't worth it." He added.

Just as he was about to leave, people with skin and hair as pale as snow appeared, and they carried the four kids forcefully.

"Where are you taking us?" Ohana shouted.

"Home." One of the pale men replied.

"Where is home? Let us go, we need to go back to our homes in the village." Maurice said.

"Don't worry, we are taking you home," another man insisted.

Finnick blacked out due to panic, and Jack remained calm and hoped he would be taken home to the village.

After a while, they arrived at a pink forest. It was beautiful, but the gases produced by the plants made the kids sleepy.

The pale men carried the kids, and they passed through a bright white light. After passing through it, the light disappeared.

When the kids woke up, they were in their houses, but the people who claimed to be their parents were different! When they demanded an explanation, their parents held a meeting where all the parents and the kids attended.

The kids were shocked! It's like they were in a new universe!

"Kids, I know this is shocking but, we are your true parents, you were stolen from us by the aliens of another multiverse on a fateful evening. Instead of returning home from a trip as you were supposed to, you all vanished without a trace! With the help of the guardians(the pale men), we were able to find you," one of the parents explained.

"How can we know what you are saying is true?" Maurice asked. "What if you are the aliens, we demand you take us back to our universe," he added.

"We know how confusing this is but we have been

looking for you for four years!" One of the parents claimed.

"How can that be? We are only seven and we can remember our first day at school together at only three years old, we have no memories of either of you," Ohana commented.

"We understand but we have accumulated evidence," One of the parents explained as he showed them their pictures as babies.

"Did your 'parents' have any baby photos of you?" He added.

The group realized their parents were right and so they went back home.

As the days passed, the kids bonded with their parents. However, they realized that they wanted to free the children stuck in the other multi-universe as well, so they carefully crafted a plan that would rescue and bring back all the children who found themselves in the wrong universe.

Since they moved to their new homes, they learned about the Moon-god, who was aware of everything happening across all multiverses. So, the kids decided to visit the Moon-god to ask for advice.

"What can we do? We want to save the remaining kids!" Maurice said.

"Yes, if someone is living a lie, we want to open their eyes!" Ohana added

The Moon-god was surprised to see how clever the kids were, so he decided to help them.

The kids were to travel to the other universe and hold a party with every child as a guest. Afterward, the portal would open, and they would all be sent back to their original home.

The following day, the kids woke up and prepared to go back to their old homes.

Their parents were a bit hesitant at first, but they eventually gave in since they understood how the other parents felt.

After being sent to their previous universe, the kids went back to their respective homes, but they were shocked to see nobody had noticed that they had disappeared. Their 'parents' went on with their regular business as usual.

Even though the situation was sad, it was more proof that they were not the kids' birth parents.

Also, it worked in the kids' favor since they had to keep a low profile.

After planning a massive party for a few days, it was time for the guests to show up. Since the kids loved to have fun, they showed up in large numbers. It was now time for Ohana, Maurice, Finnick, and Jack to wait for the portal to appear.

The party was fun, and everyone was having a good time until the kid's parents started showing up to pick them up.

Immediately, the portal sucked all the kids, and it was locked forever!

The kids were finally rescued, and the aliens didn't have a way to go to the other multiverse since it was completely sealed off.

All the kids were told what had happened, and they reunited with their families.

# FLORA

In a beautiful little town full of sunshine and warm, happy days, a girl, Amani, lived with her mother in a colorful house beneath Sunny Hill.

The house was a beauty worth marveling at since Griselda, the girl's mother, spent most of her days tending to her garden that covered their home.

The garden was so wide, and the plants covered the area around the house, making it hard to penetrate through the compound without using the main gate. As a result of this, people started making up stories in Sunny hill. They had nicknamed Griselda "Flora" after the goddess of flowering plants due to her green hands.

Everything she planted flourished and blossomed, exhibiting beauty that was never seen before. The flowers and plants were unique. The villagers loved to pass by Amani's house to look at the beautiful garden.

Griselda used her plants to heal the sick, but she mixed up the portions on an unfortunate day, making the damage irreversible. The people of Sunny hill were disappointed in her, so she locked herself in her compound for years, tending only to her plants and daughter, Amani.

Some villagers tried to climb up the garden to get into her compound during these years but could not.

"As soon as I set my eyes on her, a plant held me by my foot and threw me off the fence." One of the villagers said.

"Before I could climb the fence to make that woman pay! One of the plants spoke to me, forbidding my entry! How can a plant speak?" Another devastated villager added.

"She's a witch and we must burn her filthy garden!" One of the villagers added.

At school, the kids were curious to know if the stories were true. Everyone tried to befriend Amani to find out more about her mother.

It got to a point where she finally realized the kids at school were only being friends with her since her mother and their garden were a mystery.

"I heard that the plants at your house can speak!" One girl said!

"Yes! A plant pushed my father off your fence! Is that true?" A boy added.

"Is your mother a witch?" Another kid would rudely ask.

Instead of answering the questions, Amani kept quiet—angering the children at school more.

Each evening as Flora came from school, she'd find her mother tending to her garden.

"Mother! Is it true that the plants in our garden can speak?" she asked.

Griselda laughed hysterically and eventually answered, "What makes you say that! Plants can't talk but they can feel and that's why they respond if you care for them with love and patience," she said.

"The kids at school are saying you are a witch." Amani says.

"Oh really! Well, today I used magic to make dinner. Are you ready to taste the best pasta you've ever eaten?" Griselda says as she holds Amani's hands and the two walk-in.

"Mother! You have dirt on your hands and now it's on my uniform." Amani explained.

"Alright! Now it's on your face and hands and ears." Griselda says as she applies mad on Amani's face, hands and ears.

The two laugh and enter the dining room, where they enjoy the dinner.

"How is it? Did I tell you! Magic." Griselda says as she pretends to have a magical wand.

This makes Amani smile.

"Alright! It's time for bed!" Griselda explains.

"But mother!" Amani hesitates.

"I'll read your favorite story." Griselda adds, and Amani agrees.

While Griselda and Amani were fast asleep, smoke covered the whole compound; the villagers burned the garden!

Soon after, tiny creatures rushed to the house and tried to wake up Griselda and Amani, urging them to go where it was safe.

As Amani woke up, she couldn't believe it! There were Elves in her room!

Before asking what was going on, she fainted again due to inhaling a lot of smoke, and several elves carried her to safety.

As Amani woke up, she was in an unfamiliar place! She couldn't wrap her head around where she was! All she wanted was to see her mother.

"Where is my mother?" Amani asked.

"She's still sleeping," the elves explained.

"Where are we and why is she still sleeping." Amani asked.

"The garden is the queen's heart, she's too weak! She can only get better when the garden is revived." One of the elves explained.

"What do you mean the garden is her heart? That doesn't make sense!" Amani replied.

"Your mother is Flora, the goddess of flowering

plants. Her garden is her heart that's why she caters to it every single day. When Flora's heart is strong, the plants and flowers of the world will blossom and grow but now that she's weak, the plants will wither and die." The elf added.

"Can you take me to her?" Amani politely asked.

The elves took Amani to her mother; she was fast asleep and looked weak.

Amani tried to wake her up, but it was impossible. The elves had to help her bring back the garden to life, especially since plants from all over the world started to wither and die.

They went back to Sunny hill; it was utterly chaotic! The plants in the region had dried up, and people began to cry due to hunger!

Amani and the elves remained in their compound, and they worked silently to ensure the heart of Griselda began beating once again. This was one of the toughest things Amani had to do in her life and since the garden was completely burned down, starting from scratch wasn't easy. They failed over and over again, but they didn't give up on Griselda.

Soon after, Amani started using her mother's techniques in the garden, and a flower sprouted. After a few weeks, more flowers began to germinate while others blossomed. Eventually, Griselda opened her eyes, but she was too weak to move.

Amani and the elves had to keep trying until her

heart was truly restored. As the plants in the garden prospered, the plants in other parts of the world started sprouting.

The news that the garden of flora began to flourish once again and after, other farms started to prosper spread across the world! Suddenly people recalled the legend of Flora when her garden gave life to other gardens and forgave her actions. Eventually, Griselda woke up, and she lived happily ever after back at her home. She was happy that her daughter played a key role in making sure she remained healthy.

# THE ANTIQUE

Linda was a quiet, shy girl who loved reading old books and finding old antiques. She had learned this from her grandpa whenever she went to visit him for the holidays. She loved him with all her heart and would always write him letters about the new things she had learned in school. Linda's father was a surgeon, and she rarely saw him when she came home. Her mother would always say he was saving lives and they should be happy for the sick people getting help from papa.

Linda didn't understand why he couldn't spare some time for her. She missed him very much. On the other hand, Mother ran a small library in town, taking after the family business of Librarians. But she wasn't as fun as grandpa. She was strict about the books and arrangement systems. It made Linda learn how to be organized at a very young age, but from time to time, she would pull a few pranks on her mother that grandpa had taught her. This never ended well.

At school, Linda had a few friends; well, she didn't need many friends. She liked her best friend, Mona. She always wondered why her mother didn't wholly name her Mona Lisa. It would have been fitting for the reference to the famous painting. But Mona was no Lisa at all. She was a jolly, wild and cheeky person. She loved adventures and talking loudly.

They were a unique pair of friends, and everyone thought they were oddly fit for each other. Mona had a perfect couple of parents too. They would drop her at school together and pick her up later on in the evening. Sometimes they would offer Linda a ride home when her mother got carried away at work and forgot to pick her up.

On other days Linda would go to Mona's home, and her mom would bake them sweet chocolate cookies, and they would eat all of them with milk. But nothing came close to grandpa's cookie recipe. Mona always asked Linda to bring her a box full of them when she came back. Linda wished her parents were more like Mona's parents. She wished that they would be more present and not forget to pick her from school.

She took Mona to see her grandpa for the holidays, and it was the best summer holiday ever. Mona couldn't keep quiet from all the stories Linda's grandpa had told them. Not to mention the jars of cookies she carried. Someone might have thought she was opening a cookie shop. Mona was very good at retelling stories and exaggerating some of the details. Linda was always shy about correcting her and letting her get carried away with the story.

Linda would think of the stories grandpa narrated to her, and she would wish she was one of the characters, or maybe in a world far away, she could be one of the characters. At six years old, he had given her a locket necklace and told her not to take it off. She had always protected it, wishing maybe it had magic and waited for it to do something. She was now twelve, and nothing magical had happened yet, so she believed it was just another ordinary locket that her grandpa had gifted her.

Mona's birthday was coming up in two days, and Linda wanted to get her a perfect present. She had thought of a matching pair of lockets but couldn't get one for her friend. So she decided to go to an old antique shop in town and pick something beautiful for her friend. She drafted a quick plan on how to get to the antique shop without her mom finding out.

She never let her go anywhere without knowing about it. If it wasn't Grandpa's place, she was at Mona's place or home doing a lot of math. So she faked being sick so that her mom let her stay home. Once she heard her mother's car leave the driveway, she sprung to action. She wore her old black coat, a pair of black shades, and gloves. She was feeling like the female version of James bond.

Without wasting time, she used the back door to get out of the house, got on her bicycle, and started pedaling as fast as her little legs could go. She was very thankful that her father had bought her this bicycle for her birthday. He wasn't there to give it to her, but she still loved it. She had made a plan to get to the antique shop before her mother came back from the library.

The bicycle was not as efficient as she had hoped, but she got there at the estimated time. She was so happy and proud of herself. She parked it aside and walked inside the little shop. She was amazed by how many beautiful things she saw inside. This was even better than grandpa's place.

She had made the right decision to come here. But as she started to look for the perfect present for her friend, she got lost and indecisive about what to choose. Time was moving very fast, and she had little to spare on more sightseeing. She had to decide now, or she would end up being grounded before Mona's birthday. A nightmare!

Linda decided to ask for help from the shop owner. She walked to the front desk, where a beautiful lady was serving an old lady. She waited for them to finish speaking as she kept checking her watch. She had an hour to get back home, and the more she stood there, the more anxious she got.

"Hello Linda, how may I help you?"

"How do you know my name?"

"It's on your locket."

"Oh okay. I'm so sorry about that. I needed help picking a good present for my friend. Her birthday is coming up. But I don't know what to choose."

"I swear I have seen you before. You look like a character from my book. I was given the book by an old friend of mine."

"What does that have to do with the present?"

"Maybe I have a present for you instead."

"I don't think I understand you. Please can you help me pick a present? It's getting late, and my mom will ground me if she finds out I'm not home."

"Follow me."

Linda checked her watch one last time and followed the lady to the back of the antique shop. It was even more beautiful than the front part. Everything felt magical, like it had been drawn from a book and came to life. At the corner of the room, there was a shadow of someone with their back turned towards them. Linda suddenly felt scared of the mysterious turn of events.

She could turn around right now and run away, but her curiosity was eager to know what would happen next. The shop owner cleared her throat to signal their presence. The person turned around, and it was Mona's mom. Linda was confused to see her. There was a long silence before she decided to speak.

"I didn't expect to see you, Linda. I never expected that the chosen one was right under my nose."

"What is going Mrs. Carter?"

"I am your Guardian angel, and I'm here to take you back to your real home. Just as the prophecy foretold long eons ago."

"I want to go home now. I think I'll come another day to get a.. an antique. Thanks."

As Linda tried to walk away, the door closed itself. Then all of a sudden, so many candles lit up and filled the room with light. Linda tried to scream, but no words came out of her mouth.

"Listen to me carefully child, your real home is in grave danger and you are needed. You are the savior and we don't have much time. This world is not your home. That locket necklace your grandfather gave to you is the key to getting back home."

"But I don't know anything about magic Mrs. Carter."

"I think your Grandfather has prepared you well. So are you ready to go?"

Linda nodded her head. But before anything happened, she asked if she could write her friend a letter for her birthday. Mrs. Carter magically created a letter and a pen from thin air. Linda still couldn't believe everything that was happening. She sat down on a little chair next to the shop owner, who had not spoken since they got inside the room. She didn't know what to write and decided to wish her a happy birthday instead.

*Dear Mona,*

*My grandfather has summoned me to go to see him. It is very important. I am so sorry I won't be around for your birthday; I have you in my thoughts wherever I go. I hope my present will be perfect for your beautiful day—lots of cookies and hugs. Happy birthday Mona. I love you, my dear friend.*

*Linda.*

As Linda arrived at Starlight, she had to lead a new life that would go hand in hand with her duties. She had to forget her previous life and dedicate herself to the battle.

As days passed, she started missing her old home, and most of all, she missed her best friend, Mona. Linda decided to work harder than ever before to be allowed to bring Mona to Starlight as a wish.

Linda grew stronger through each passing day, and her people believed she would reign as a good leader. Finally, it was the day of the battle, and after putting up a tough fight, she won and was able to bring her best friend with her to Starlight—their reunion proved to Linda that all she needed was a good friend to get the will to fight for a good life.

## HAKIM

In a tiny little village, there lived an orphan boy. He had strange blue hair and a pale white face that was as white as snow. He also wore an old cloak that glowed at night. Most people feared him and never talked to him. Whispers would go around town saying he was the son of a wizard, and whoever dared to go near him would turn into salt or snow. The little boy never spoke to anyone either and despised humans. He lived at the edge of the river banks and would often be seen sailing his boat and fishing.

His name was Hakim, but most villagers preferred to call him the Lost Boy. Hakim was a beautiful boy, and all the girls in the village would be seen waving at him at the river banks for his attention. But Hakim would not even look at them as he continued to row his boat to a favorite spot he liked to fish. He would catch so many fish and give some to the tiny orphans at the river. But still, he never spoke to anyone. He was a strange boy, and as years went by, everyone got used to him. A few remained curious about where he came from.

One day as Hakim was fishing, he came across a strange box wrapped in chains. He decided to take it back to his little hut by the river and see what was inside. This was the first time something exciting had happened since his father left him a message and disappeared two days later. That day still haunted him, and he carried the letter wherever he went. The letter was written in a strange language he could not understand. He missed his father so much, and he felt like he needed to find him.

As Hakim tried to open the box, he found it locked with a unique padlock. There were words written on the padlock that looked similar to the ones in his father's letter. Hakim was very frustrated and kicked the box away. He wanted to cry out, but a thought came to mind. He rushed and took the box and laid it in front of him. He took his father's letter and tried to recite the strange words as he saw them. Slowly the padlock started unlocking with every incantation of his words. Hakim was very excited and nervous. What if he found something else that would not help him find his father? What if it was not meant to be opened?

Hakim breathed slowly and removed the chains

covering the box, and slowly lifted the top. His eyes widened with mystery and joy. Inside the box were tools and letters. He took the little box and placed it on a table to study the contents. He removed all the strange-looking tools and set them aside. And then he took the letters. A strong wind came rushing into the house and almost blew the letters away. Hakim ran to the door and closed it and also his window. He thought to himself how that was weird and strange. He gathered the scattered letters and tried to arrange them. But he could not remember the order. Luckily for him, the letters were written in English, and he could read and understand the words.

*"Dear son,*

*I have traveled far and wide in search of the elixir of life. I have made friends and enemies in equal measures. Forgive me for not explaining everything to you. But remember, everything I taught you will help you survive the gulags. They are very vicious. These letters will guide you. Be careful because the wind summons strange things at night.*

*Lord Belzar."*

This was a letter from his father. Hakim tried to read it three times to understand what his father was trying to tell him, but he could not. He was so angry. Where was he? Was he still alive? What is a gulag? He sat down on his small chair and closed his eyes. He tried to remember his childhood memories and how his father looked. It had been so long, and he was just a lonely, sad boy.

"Teach me how to be like you, father." Hakim would say.

"Listen to the winds my boy, the winds will guide you to the secrets of the mountain." His father replied.

"I don't hear anything." Hakim would insist.

"That's because your mind is closed to the surroundings. Try to breathe in and calm yourself. Then feel it in your heart." His father explained.

"I can feel..I can't feel anything papa." Hakim went on and on.

Lord Belzar laughs.

"When you're a bit older you will, my son. Patience." His father would reply.

Hakim breathed in slowly as the memory of his father faded away. He made up his mind to find his father. The rest of the letters were maps to the mountains of Argoth. They were dangerous and guarded by thorns at the foot of the mountain. Many had died trying to climb it. One letter had instructions on what the strange tools were for.

His father had prepared him for this journey, and he was terrified of what lay ahead. That night Hakim packed his traveling bag for a long journey ahead. He wore his special robe that his mother had made him for protection. Beneath was his soldier's armor that was a common symbol of rank. He was the son of a king in his other life, but he didn't want anyone to know about it. But now, he felt the urge to honor his father by wearing his former uniform.

At dawn, Hakim rowed his boats and left the little village behind him. This was the last time they would see him. He left a note at his door; whoever reads it could have the small hut to themselves. He didn't need it anymore. As the village disappeared from his sight, he felt a cold rush of wind. The river separated itself into three parts: one going east, the other north, and the last one west. The map didn't show the river. And then he thought of his father's words; *"listen to the winds my boy."*

Hakim closed his eyes and thought of his father, and then he breathed in deeply and listened to the wind. It seemed to whisper to him. He could hear it faintly telling him to go North. He rowed his boat north and hoped he had made the right decision. Dark clouds started forming from afar, and he knew he had to row faster before the storm caught up with hIm.

As he was about to turn the sail, he saw something from the corner of his eye. Shadows were hiding in the bushes. Hakim was afraid, but he had his weapon in his pocket and continued to row his boat. The tides started changing as the downpour began increasing. He couldn't go to the dry land as the shadows emerged from the bushes and revealed themselves as the most frightening creatures he had ever seen. They were the gulags. Hakim thought he was safe, but the gulags started walking towards the water and diving in. He was terrified.

His boat was also filling in the water, and he had to act fast. He decided to use some enchantments his mother had taught him to scare away the gulags. He closed his eyes and recited the words, and a bright light filled the sky. The gulags cried out loud in fear. Then Hakim jumped into the water and let the current take him. He could see the gulags tearing apart the little boat from a distance as they looked for him. For now, he was safe, but the current was becoming stronger, and he started choking on the water. He tried to grasp on anything but failed as the water kept swallowing him until he couldn't breathe anymore. And everything went dark.

Hakim could hear sounds of creatures and people, but his body was heavy, and his eyes felt like they had glue. He felt helpless and weak. Then memories of his mother singing to him would come to mind, and then his father smiling at her. He missed them both. He drifted from one dream to another, but the sounds never went away. When Hakim came back to his senses, he was surrounded by people he didn't know. He tried to wake up, but his legs were tied, and so were his hands.

"Who are you? Where am I?"

But the people kept staring at him, not moving an

inch. And as he was about to ask them again, a loud cry was heard from behind him. He tried to turn but he couldn't. Hakim was now scared and started shivering. The two people came and raised him on his feet so that he could see what was coming. He could not believe his eyes. It was his Father but as one of the gulags.

"Welcome home son," he said.

# AIYANA

In a cheerful town where the days were always warm and the skies blue. There lived a special girl called Aiyana. She was the kindest kid in her neighborhood. Everyone admired how caring she was—if anyone was in trouble, she tried her best to solve the problem.

Since she was as clever as a fox, she created unique solutions, gaining the admiration of the people in her community at a young age.

What made Aiyana stand out from the rest was her selflessness and kindness.

Aiyana's father, George, was a doctor. He cured a lot of people in the village. All his patients praised him since he was good at his job. Also, like his daughter—he was a kind man!

Her mother was a nurse but died shortly after she

was infected with an unknown disease. This pushed Aiyana to learn more about Medicine to find a cure for the rarest diseases.

Aiyana followed in her father's footsteps; she was a quick learner and a free thinker. She thought about everything and never left any important details behind.

Even at a young age, medicine interested her. She took care of her friends' wounds whenever they fell while playing in the field.

Naturally, Aiyana started her journey towards becoming a Doctor at a young age. She made frequent visits to the hospital with her father to learn all about Anatomy.

On a fateful day, as she was with her father at work, she was able to help him find a way to calm a kid that was about to go for surgery. She explained that he was in good hands.

Her talking skills were helpful, and the kid had a successful surgery.

As Aiyana grew, she was able to learn more about medicine.

Everyone referred to her as "Doctor" even though she was still in school and had never set foot in a College. Her future was bright.

Even when she was young, her wonderful work was admired by all around her.

But no matter how hardworking she was, Aiyana was

still a dreamer at heart. She remembered how her mother once said, "If you want your dreams to come true, whisper your wishes to the star and their light will lead the way!"

So every night, she'd sit outside and look at the stars.

Ever so often, she'd hope the stars would grant her wish.

"I wish to become the best doctor in the whole region," She politely said.

"I'd really love to shine on those I love." She added on.

After saying this, the largest star in the group of stars twinkled brightly.

After practicing at the hospital with her father, she went back home.

To keep her mother's dream alive, the following night, she'd sit at her window, admiring the stars, and politely whisper, "I wish to become the best doctor in the whole country."

The largest star twinkled once again.

Slowly by slowly, it became a habit, and every single night, Aiyana went to see the stars to ask them to grant her wish after her medical practice with her father.

Years passed, and she blossomed into a beautiful young woman but still, every night, she asked the stars to grant her wish.

All she wanted was to manifest her purpose and align her destiny with the Universe.

Aiyana was a bright girl, and so she graduated high school and went to nursing school in the capital city.

After a few years of working hard, she came back to her hometown to help the sick.

Everyone in the town was proud of her.

Aiyana always helped those who could not pay for medicine by treating them for free.

Her heart was truly made of gold.

The children and the elderly loved her since she was patient and understanding while treating them.

She had just helped a boy who broke his arm while playing soccer and an older man who couldn't walk, and both families were thankful.

The people close to Aiyana believed she was a genius since her way of solving health problems was unique but still worked as well as the other ways.

But, sometimes, the nicest people go through unkind situations even though they deserve all the goodness the world can give.

After a few months, a terrible disease began spreading all over the world.

Aiyana bid her family goodbye because she had to go back to the capital to help prevent the disease from spreading further.

The doctors couldn't understand why everyone was

getting sick! It was a mystery to them because the disease was unheard of!

As Aiyana arrived in the town, she couldn't believe her eyes.

The disease had spread all over the city.

Everyone was suffering.

The doctors and the nurses held a meeting to try and find a cure.

Aiyana and her team spent countless nights finding a cure, but their efforts bore no fruits each time.

This didn't make her lose hope.

It just made her stronger despite the hardships she faced at the hospital.

Aiyana and her team had to find a cure fast!

Since Aiyana cared about everyone in her country, these horrible circumstances pushed her to develop unique solutions to find a cure.

Aiyana read different books, both ancient and modern texts, to find a cure.

On a fateful night, as everyone was asleep, Aiyana woke up and sat by the window.

She looked at the sky, but the city lights were too bright, so she couldn't see the stars.

The moon shone alone in the pitch-black sky.

"I wish to find a cure to help my people." Aiyana politely asked.

The same star that was brighter than the rest twinkled.

Not long after, she fell asleep.

Aiyana had a vivid dream; she remembered how she got sick when she was younger, and her grandmother would mix herbs and a special purple flower to cure her.

"Aiyana, the universe blessed us with the trees because they can heal us. That is why you should always respect the trees and take care of the universe." Her grandmother insisted.

As Aiyana woke up in the morning, she couldn't tell whether it was a dream or her grandmother was there. It felt so real.

But at least, this time, she had a solution that could help everyone.

She didn't go to work on that day but chose to go to the forest that surrounded the city to look for the magical purple flowers.

She wandered through the forest for hours, yet she couldn't find the flowers.

Aiyana had to sit and think clearly.

"Where can I find these flowers?" She asked herself.

A few minutes later, she saw a bright ray of light shining through the sky and falling upon weeds that were scattered around a tall tree.

She chose to trust the sign and went where the light had shone.

As she uncovered the weeds, she found the magical flowers.

Aiyana was happy that her efforts were fruitful, and so she went back to the hospital.

Aiyana suggested the other doctors should use the flower to find a cure. At first, they all refused to believe it, and this made Aiyana furious.

She stormed out of the conference room, went to the lab, and began creating a cure on her own.

After a few days, Aiyana began giving the patients drops of the syrup in the flowers, and the sickness went away.

After a week of being helped by other doctors to give the syrup to the patients, the disease was wiped off completely.

Most of the doctors were surprised. How could a flower heal a disease when medicine couldn't! Most of them asked Aiyana this question, and she told them that the trees are healers and everyone should take care of the environment.

Aiyana was celebrated as a hero in the city, her small town, and the whole world.

She had been able to save many lives thanks to her faith and spirit of never giving up.

In the end, Aiyana proved to be as valuable to human health as a doctor. After the doctors followed her advice, the disease was wiped off!

Her abilities amazed the whole world, and she was appointed as the head doctor.

As she went back home, she spoke to the stars like she always has, "Dear stars, thank you for granting my wishes!"

After this, Aiyana continued her dream of becoming the best doctor in the world. Following in her father's footsteps, Aiyana made his mark as a great doctor.

She didn't just go by the book!

Aiyana had a unique way of doing things.

She was an all-rounded woman who believed that plants were medicine.

Her curiosity, hard work, and willingness to try different ways brought Aiyana many opportunities.

During Aiyana's adventures to different parts of the world, she learned different types of medicine and how to heal people using them.

One of the most important journeys of her life began on a fateful day when she had lost her way back home after the ship she was using wrecked.

This journey was difficult, but it still shaped her into the best doctor in the world.

To survive the wreckage, Aiyana and the crew had to swim towards a rocky island.

As they arrived, they realized that there was no way to go back home—some people had injuries. Also, all the food was destroyed on the ship. Nobody knew how they were going to survive this horrible ordeal.

On the bright side, Aiyana assisted the people who were injured using her skills. She catered to their wounds until they felt better.

The next day, the sun rose brightly, just as any other day. The crew woke Aiyana up and asked her how they were going to survive.

Aiyana was shocked to see that people depended on her. They trusted her because of how she helped those in need after the Ship's wreckage.

This time, she had to step up her leadership skills while still taking care of the health of those around her.

Aiyana was a kind and selfless person, and so taking care of others wasn't tricky.

The crew decided to stick with Aiyana during the hard time to make it a bit easier. They hoped another ship would approach, and they would all aboard and leave to safety and have access to basic needs, but that didn't happen, the hours became days, and the days became months.

Through each passing day, the crew grew weary and tired.

The rocky island was hard to survive in because of the scorching sun during the day. But—at least Aiyana's knowledge of plants and medicine allowed them to find food and medicine.

On a fateful day, as Aiyana was walking around the Island trying to find plants to make food and medicine, she stumbled upon a rare plant. She took it back with her and stored it somewhere safe.

She catered to her duties as she always would, but this time, something was different. She saw a wounded animal on the ground. Her love for the environment and animals wouldn't allow her to leave the poor creature unattended.

Besides, there were no creatures on the Island, and so this was a rare occurrence. She tried to understand how the creature could enter the Island but couldn't come up with answers.

She took the animal with her and ran shallow tests since she didn't have her medical equipment. Soon, she realized that the creature could only survive in that area if there were grains on the island, but *where were these grains?*

Aiyana made a medicine concoction and fed the animal. She went outside, freed it, and began following it to see where it went. Soon after, it led her to a Cave. She was shocked! She had never seen the Cave before!

As she went in, she noticed that the creature was not limping anymore. It ran instead. Also, she noticed that there were a lot of flowers — like the one she picked before.

*Could the flower's pollen have healed the animal?*

She collected the flowers and tried to use them on some of the wounded crewmembers, and a miracle happened! They were completely healed! No scars were showing that there was a sign of sickness or injury.

This was a shocking discovery, and so she continued to research more about the flowers and collected them.

After a few days, a Ship passed nearby. The crew members raised flashy items, and they were rescued.

Aiyana's discovery saved many lives and prevented diseases. She was praised for using plants to find cures and food. Her practices were enough to allow humans to live long and healthy lives.

Until today, Aiyana is seen as the best doctor in the world. She is mainly remembered for her playful heart, making wishes on stars, and her witty brain.

## SPY ADVENTURES OF DORY AND LORY

On a Sunny hill where the days are always warm and the skies blue, there was a quaint house home to Dory and his family. Dory was the most intelligent and clumsiest boy in Sunny hill. The sun fell away and rested for a while. The following day it rose and shone brightly, casting golden rays through Dory's bedroom window, waking him up to prepare for his first day at school.

Dory makes his way downstairs to eat breakfast.

"The last one to finish his or her breakfast is a rotten Potato," Lory, Dory's twin sister, yells as she takes a big bite of her blueberry pancakes.

"Okay, but don't say I didn't warn you I'd be the winner," Dory replies as he takes a bigger bite of his pancakes. "Kids? What did I say about playing during breakfast? What if one of you chokes?" The twins' mom, Sara, asked.

"DONE!" Lory yells. "As always, I win!"

"Not true, you started eating before me! Mom! Mom! Lory is a cheater!" Dory cries.

"Enough! Both of you are winners!" their mom says.

She drove the kids to school and dropped them. On their way to class, the kids stumbled upon a man who wore a Jetpack.

"I have been looking for you the whole day! You are late for your first mission," the man said as he carried the twins, and they flew away.

At the time, Dory and Lory didn't understand what was going on, but it seemed fun, so they decided to withhold the information that they weren't who the man was looking for.

As they arrived, the man gave them pass tags and told them he'd meet them later.

They were impressed at how big and cool it was. They stood outside the huge school, and a voice of an unknown woman said, "To acquire access, verify ID." The twins placed their IDs on the sensor at the same time, and the door opened. As they entered the school, the twins were more amazed.

"Kids! You are late! Where have you been? You need to go on a mission in a few minutes" A man approached them and explained.

The twins agreed, but they didn't know about the mission—they were just here to have fun even though they didn't understand what was going on.

"The work you'll be doing is top-secret. I can't disclose anything as of now but you have to go on your first mission." The man explained.

"What is our first mission?" Lory asks excitedly.

"Your first mission will be going back in time using a time machine. This mission is top secret! There is a villain known as Cornelius who is turning people into Zombies. There is a valuable Dinosaur bone that you need to find. That Dinosaur bone is our only hope for turning the Zombies back to humans." The man in black explains. The twins listen to him quietly.

"If you have any questions, I'm here to answer them." The man adds on.

The twins didn't understand why they were being sent on a mission to the past, but since it was more fun than regular classes, they accepted the offer.

The twins were dressed in black tuxedos, carried their bags packed with Spy mission essentials, and stood in front of the Time machine that took them back when the Dinosaurs still existed.

Dory peers through his binoculars at the Horizon. He spots the targets and whispers, "I see them, there are many Dinosaurs, we can't pass through all of them! We don't stand a chance. Here look," He gives Lory the binoculars.

"Why did we have to agree!" Dory adds. "Relax! This is an adventure of a lifetime! Just try to enjoy it," she said.

As Lory looks through the Binoculars, Dory says, "I have an idea! We'll pass through the Dinosaurs without being noticed. Just change and wear camouflage," he said.

They took a dinosaur bone on the ground, but as they tried to escape, a dinosaur spotted them, and several started chasing after them.

"Oh! Oh! Why do I hear a stampede behind us?" Lory asks.

"RUN!!!!!!" Dory shouts as the two begin to run as fast as they can. They arrive at the Time machine, and Dory presses a button to take them back to the present time, but each time they end up at different times!

"Why is the machine not working! Why do we end up at different times? Did you press the green button or the red button?" Lory asks angrily.

"We had an emergency and tough times called for tough solutions. I just pressed a button! I'm sorry!" Dory says as he begins to cry. "We should have just gone to school!" he adds.

Lory feels terrible for shouting at Dory, and so she faces him and starts saying, "You know, you're the smartest kid in the whole world! I'm sorry for shouting at you."

Dory stops sobbing and says, "It's okay, you're my sister, and I love you."

"I love you too, Dory," Lory replies as they hug.

"But, can you find a solution fast before we get stuck in time?" Lory suggests.

Dory immediately realizes that the green button is stuck, so he fixes it, and they directly arrive at the school.

"What took you so long! We were worried! Did you succeed?" The man asks.

"Yes, we did, but we don't have any time to lose. It's now or never! Here is the dinosaur Bone." Dory replies.

"We will send you to another mission. If the mission is too hard, you can simply find your way out and call for help using your communicator watches. Do you understand?" Asked the man in black.

"Yes!" The twins reply at the same time.

The head boy walks into the room and greets them. The three set out for the mission using their Jetpacks.

As soon as they arrive, they realize that hundreds of people have been infected and have become Zombies.

The three pull-out guns that have been infused with Dinosaur bone juice. They stay in position and wait to ambush the Zombies.

Lory and Dory stick together while the head boy hides in another position. As the Zombies make their way near the three Spies, they begin shooting them with guns. As they attack the Zombies, they become humans again.

Cornelius, the villain, notices that his army of Zombies is being converted into humans, so he turns off all the lights. That way, the Zombies would have a winning advantage by attacking the three spies since they couldn't see in the dark.

Dory had some tricks up his sleeves, and so he removed night vision glasses from his Jetpack and continued fighting the Zombies all on his own. He realized the only way to turn all the Zombies back to being humans was to turn their leader, Cornelius.

He goes to where Lory and the head boy are hiding and tells them to set up a trap for Cornelius. He gives them spare Night vision glasses, and the three manage to turn Cornelius into a human being. Soon after, all the Zombies are turned into human beings.

Since Dory was patient and intelligent, he could save the world during his first mission with his sister and a new friend's help.

Later on, the kids realized they had accidentally joined a spy kids program, but they were given a badge to join the network due to their diligence and hard work. After a while in the program, they became the best spies in the entire world.

## COSMO, THE DETECTIVE

I t was a beautiful summer day at Butterfly beach. The sun shone brightly, making the water in the sea glitter. Everyone was happy and cheerful in the quaint little town except Cosmo, he had solved every case, and it was time for his next adventure! Cosmo had adapted to his new friends, and finally, it was time to say goodbye. Cosmo packed his belongings, ready to travel to Italy.

He visited his new friends, bid them goodbye, and went straight to the train station. As much as he was a little sad, he was still excited for his new adventure and ready to solve any mysteries.

He boarded the train and sat by the window! Cosmo was a dreamer and loved to view things from a deeper point of view; he believed everything, even the smallest things were meaningful—this perspective helped him solve a lot of cases since he didn't ignore even the slightest hints.

Suddenly, he fell asleep but was soon woken up by loud screams!

*Who is in trouble! I need to see how I can help!*

As soon as Cosmo woke up, he noticed that a woman with long dark hair was screaming because she had misplaced her keys. At this time, he believed he would be able to solve the case!

"I'm sorry Miss, where were you last before you entered the train and who was beside you?" Cosmo asked, hoping to find clues.

"I entered the train using the entrance door! I can't remember who was close to me!" She explained.

"Alright!" Said Cosmo.

Even though the clue wasn't strong enough to find a lead, he still went to the entrance to check whether he could find the woman's keys.

As he arrived, he looked everywhere but still couldn't find them!

"Who walked in with this woman on the train?" Cosmo asked, but nobody replied—maybe because one of them was the prime suspect or, no one took the woman's keys.

He had to look into both perspectives to find the woman's keys.

Immediately after, he searched the train, but nobody had the keys!

The problem had to be the woman because no one had stolen the necklace.

After realizing this, he told her to stand up because the keys might have been in her clothes. As soon as she stood up, keys started to jingle but still, he couldn't find where they were!

Cosmo had one way to solve the mystery! The woman had to jump up and down. At first, she refused but agreed later on, and her keys fell out of her long dark hair.

The woman thanked her, and Cosmo retired to his seat, hoping they would arrive in Italy in the next few hours!

Soon after, the plane finally landed! Cosmos was happy and hopped out as fast as possible, hoping to find more cases to solve throughout Italy.

As Cosmo walked through the streets of Italy, he was amazed by the smell of pasta that filled the air!

He also enjoyed the lovely views on the rooftop.

The city was sunny and beautiful.

Since Cosmo wanted to visit his friend, John, who worked at a Pizza restaurant, he went straight to the restaurant.

As he walked through the hallways of the restaurant with his friend, John, he could sense that something wasn't right!

And once he asked John, he told him that the Chef had lost his hat.

This was the perfect opportunity to use his witty mind to find the culprit.

And so, John took Cosmo to the crime scene.

As Cosmo arrived at the crime scene, he began to look for clues.

"Who would've stolen the Chef's hat?" Asks John.

"Well, we're about to find out." Says Cosmo.

Cosmo was hot on the trail.

He vowed to find the suspects and eventually solve the case.

As he continued to look around, he noticed footprints that led to a dark tunnel.

"Are you sure about this?" Asked John—he didn't want to get in more trouble.

"You don't have to follow the footprints John, I can solve the case on my own and help the Chef." Cosmo says.

"Of course not—I'm here for you, my friend!" John replies.

"So, where do we start?" Asks John.

"Well, as far as I know, this cheeky suspect doesn't live in the Restaurant." Says Cosmo.

"How do you know? And, where can we find him?" Asks John.

"Patience, my dear friend! First, let's follow the footprints." Cosmo replies.

John is a bit scared—well, that was to be expected.

But they continued to go further into the tunnel.

As they arrived at the far end, they bumped into a lot of mice.

One of them held the Chef's hat.

Immediately, the mice disappeared and dropped the hat on the floor, and escaped.

Cosmo's first mission in Italy was complete; he found the Chef's hat and returned it.

It was time to bid John goodbye and go somewhere else to solve more crimes! Cosmo decided to go to his old school to meet the new students who checked in to see if he could help out in any way. Cosmo wandered through the streets of Rome.

Everyone was in a hurry—well, except Cosmo, who admired the city. The skies were clear, it was a beautiful day, but the sun was setting soon, and he had to arrive at his destination as quickly as possible.

He went back to the Marina Riviera school of boys, where he was warmly received.

As he arrived, he couldn't help but notice that something was off.

The boys were awfully sad—when he was still a young lad, he was happy because he could go on adventures with his friends, but that was not the case for the boys at the school.

He started looking for clues without anyone noticing and tried to ask some of the boys what the problem was, but nobody answered!

It was time to solve the second mystery of the day.

Cosmo tried to follow the boys to the field, but that didn't work.

They didn't even try to play ball. They seemed tired all day long, as if they didn't get enough rest throughout the night.

*Why are the boys sad and uneasy! How can I find the problem then the solution?*

These thoughts ran across Cosmo's mind.

"This culprit is smarter than everyone I have dealt with before." He says to himself.

"What are you babbling about?" His old friend Jason asked as he started laughing.

"Nothing really, just focusing on the clues." Cosmo replies.

"It seems like you never shed off your detective side, you're still good at this. Well, I'll be in the field if you need me." Says Jason.

Jason worked in the school as the chef despite studying in the same school.

As Jason leaves, Cosmo realizes that the boys could be tired because of the food they are being fed, and so he follows him to the kitchen to watch him cook.

He didn't believe that Jason could harm even a fly, but looks can be somewhat deceiving. Regardless, Cosmo didn't want to jump to conclusions. He had to be sure first.

Cosmo entered the kitchen and watched Jason

cook; he looked at his ingredients to get more clues. But everything he did seemed pretty normal.

Cosmo tried to brush it off, but if Jason was the one causing the problem, it was bound to be found out!

Just when Jason walked away, Cosmo took some of the food and went back to his room at the school to find out whether the food was the problem, or the boys were less energetic compared to him when he was a young boy!

As soon as he looked at the food particles in his microscope, he realized that something was wrong, but how could his closest friend do this to the children at school! They were so tired—they looked like Zombies throughout the day. How could they grasp anything during class!

Cosmo decided to confront Jason about the matter, but he was utterly shocked as well. He didn't understand who added sleeping pills to the food!

Cosmo and Jason decided to find the culprit who wanted to see the prestigious Marina Riviera school fail.

As they were heading back to the kitchen, they saw the principal add chamomile to the food. This would make the boys dizzy throughout the day. They immediately reported him to the local authorities, and he was taken to the police station, where he was charged.

On the other hand, the boys recovered, and the

school went back to its glory and started leading in the whole region.

Cosmo had solved another important case, and it was time for his next adventure in the city of Rome. He bid Jason goodbye and took the next step.

# THE MAGICAL INVENTORS

In a colorful town, where the days were always warm and the skies blue, two smart yet clumsy kids lived in a rainbow house on top of a hill; their names were Liloo and Lilaa.

Liloo wasn't as talkative or expressive as Lilaa, but his strength lay in inventing helpful machines; that's how he expressed his skills.

Lilaa wasn't as analytical as Liloo, but she was curious and quick to act. Their uniqueness balanced out their skills and made them a strong team.

The twins were fascinated by Science and found adventurous ways to learn in unusual yet fun ways.

Alone in their attic, they built machines and gadgets that they loved.

After finishing the experiments, they would hide their machines somewhere no one could find.

At home, they would build fine inventions to make their family's life easier.

"Liloo! Lilaa! Why can the alarm clock scream!" Their father exclaimed.

"So you'll never be late at work ," they said, "Gee! Thanks kids!" Their father replied as he flew up in the air and far, far away.

Liloo and Lilaa were inspired by their great grandfather, Pako, a great Aerospace engineer who built airplanes and spacecraft a long time ago!

Every night before bedtime, they would ask their mother to tell them more stories about Grandpa Pako!

"I want to be like Grandpa!" Liloo said. "Me too! He was a great engineer!" Lilaa added.

"Alright Kids! I'll tell you a story about Grandpa Pako!" Their mother said.

But before she reached the middle of the story, the kids were deep in slumber—they were tired from making inventions throughout the day!

After science class, the twins would politely ask their teacher, Mrs. Shelley, for any tools or engineering treasures to add to their hideaway.

"Mrs. Shelley, do you have any treasures for us today?" The twins would ask politely.

If Mrs. Shelley had them, she'd give them without a second thought! She believed the twins were special, and one day they would become great scientists.

"Unfortunately, I have no treasures today but you can come tomorrow," she replied.

"Thank you Mrs. Shelley!" The kids responded.

Since Liloo and Lilaa had big dreams, they started checking off the goals on their list at a young age.

Their next goal was to join the famous School of Inventors.

On a chilly night, the moon shone high above. The kids went to their attic to discuss an invention to build to send to the Space station.

"I believe we can build a great machine! The scientist would be happy to welcome us. We can do it, Liloo," Lilaa insisted.

"I don't know what to build!" Liloo says.

"We are a team! I'll help you come up with ideas for the project," Lilaa explains.

Since it was getting late, the kids retired to bed.

That night, Liloo and Lilaa couldn't sleep a wink!

This project would be one of the most important inventions they had ever made — It had to be mind-blowing!

Suddenly, a bold idea popped up in Lilaa's mind.

*Could she help Liloo build an invention that could be launched to space!*

Some inventions are tricky to make,

This one kept Lilaa wide awake,

And at the break of dawn,

She knew what to do!

After school, the kids went to their attic to build a rocket that would fly to outer space on that special day.

They worked throughout the day and tested their rocket outside to see if it could fly.

They launched the rocket, and it flew high up in the sky. To ensure it didn't go far since they had to send it to the school of inventions, Liloo jumped and caught it.

"The machine is set! We will send it tomorrow," Liloo said as he gave Liloo a high five.

The following day arrived, and as they woke up to send their invention, they realized the Rocket had turned into a real Spacecraft.

They stood perplexed and didn't quite understand what was happening!

*Was it magic? How could magic and science go hand in hand!*

Regardless, the kids still wanted to achieve their dreams, so they sent the gizmo to the school of inventions.

They waited for a response but nothing came up.

Just when they were about to give up, something interesting happened!

They received an invitation letter to the school of inventions from a man in black.

The kids were beyond excited!

"Mom! Dad! We'll finally be like Grandpa!" They said excitedly.

"We are so proud of you!" Their parents assured them.

That night, the kids couldn't sleep! It felt like they were floating on air.

The following day arrived pretty quickly. The sun shone, casting golden rays in the twin's bedroom. They woke up and prepared for their journey to the space station.

Soon after, a driver from the school picked them up.

They bid their parents goodbye and headed to the airport.

The kids couldn't wrap their heads around what was happening, they knew it was happening, but it still didn't register clearly in their little yet smart brains.

Their lives would finally change for the good!

As they arrived at the airport, they were mesmerized by how large the planes were.

As they waited for their plane to arrive, the driver gave them Space passes that they would use at the Space station and a band watch to gain their abilities at the Space station and left them in the care of a tall man wearing a black tuxedo.

The kids accepted the letter because they would test out their rocket at the school of inventions. They would finally find out how their Rocket gizmo turned into a real rocket that could fly to outer space. Their main objective was to discover if magic existed in the real world.

Soon after, their plane arrived and took them straight to the school of inventions.

The kids arrived, and they decided to conduct more studies on their rocket.

So during their free time, the duo snuck into the launch control center and tried their luck, but nothing out of the ordinary happened—machines were simply based on science, not magic.

The twins decided to focus on other lessons in the meantime.

Since it was their second lesson, their teacher, Mr. Sherman, an inventor, and engineer, trusted them to start by researching on their own. If they succeed at this lesson, it will show that they can handle almost anything on their own—everyone knows that scientists are great team leaders.

At the end of the lesson, Mr. Sherman introduced a science contest.

The team that would make a great experiment would win prizes.

The twins went to the lab to discuss the upcoming project.

"We need to build an interesting experiment that would make us win the prize!" Lilaa insisted.

"I agree!" Liloo said.

"What would mother say about Grandpa when he wasn't sure about his next invention." Lilaa asked.

"He would take some time off to stay alone." Liloo answered.

"Yes! That's what we should do." Lilaa said.

The duo decided to rest. They had three days to come up with a winning experiment.

Days passed, and the duo came up with a gizmo. They decided to build a robot. The idea was great, but it needed teamwork and cooperation, but after a while, they were successful.

As they went to bed and woke up early in the morning to prepare their gizmo, they couldn't find the robot where they had left it. That's when they returned to their rooms and found it sitting on their bed!

The twins were shocked; they didn't understand why suddenly, their inventions were coming to life!

So, the kids decided to return home to ask their parents if this occurred to their grandfather, Pako.

"Kids! Where are you getting these ideas?" Their mother asked.

Suddenly they let the robot in. The twin's mother was shocked to see the robot standing in their living room.

She knew she had to contact his father as soon as possible to find answers.

Grandpa Pako was an unusual and unpredictable man; no one knew what to expect from him because he had a lot of tricks up his sleeves!

The following day, he flew to the house using a hot

air balloon! The twins were so happy to see him,, but they were also ready to ask him how their gizmos began coming to life.

"You summoned me, here I am! I brought you the best vanilla ice cream you'll ever eat!" Pako explained.

"But grandpa! It's already melted!" Lilaa exclaimed.

"Not with this machine I built!" Pako insisted.

The kids took the ice cream and went to enjoy it. The twin's mother sat down with her father and asked him why the twin's inventions were coming to life!

At first, he denied the theory—saying it was untrue and the kids just had a creative imagination, but after looking at his daughter's eyes, he knew he had to come clean.

"We are a family of magical inventors! Everything we build comes to life." Pako explained.

The twins found out, and this strengthened their passion for inventing things. They kept the robot, and he helped them with their gizmos at school.

# HOW THE WINTER CAME BY

Before time was time, On a Sunny hill where days were always warm and the skies blue, there lived a Jaguar.

The Jaguar spent his time trying to find food, but he was not as successful as the Fox, so he asked the Fox for food.

"If you spare me some meat, I'll let you eat in peace tomorrow." Said the hungry Jaguar.

"Here!" Said the Fox as she threw some of the meat to the Jaguar.

"Th-Thankyou Fox!" Says the hungry Jaguar as he rushed to catch the meat as it fell from the sky.

"Learn to look for your own food because tomorrow I won't be so kind." The Fox adds on as she flys away.

"Mmh, delicious! But tomorrow I'll have to look for

my own food because Fox won't be so generous!" The Jaguar says to himself as he eats the meat.

The sun fell away and rested for a while. It rose and shone the following day brightly, casting golden rays on Jaguar's face, waking him up to get ready for his first hunting trip. As we walked through the river, he noticed how the sun made the river glitter—he thought it was beautiful.

The fish jumped up and down on the blue river, playing peek-a-boo with the birds in the Sky. The day was warm, so the Jaguar decided to nap under the giant tree. Time went by, and it was nighttime. The Jaguar woke up only to find out the day passed by as he was sleeping. That night the Jaguar slept hungrily.

As the Jaguar woke up the next day, he swore to find some food to eat. While the Jaguar was walking through the forest, he saw the blue sky open and butterflies emerging from the sky, flying towards Sunny hill. He loved what he saw, and so he went on top of the hill and observed, admiring and cheering.

After a few minutes, the Fox flew directly towards the Jaguar and said, "Instead of looking for food to eat, you just sit around, doing nothing all day long? Tonight don't come near my nest."

She immediately flew away before Jaguar got a chance to speak.

Fox's words hurt Jaguar, and so he went hunting. Jaguar wanted to eat fish, and so he went to the river.

As the Jaguar arrived at the deep blue river, he noticed that the fishes jumped up and down in the water. He hid behind the shrubs and waited until a fish jumped up to snatch it from the river. After waiting for a few minutes, the perfect opportunity arrived, and he managed to catch a fish. Jaguar was very happy! It had been so long ever since he was able to hunt successfully.

As the fish gasped for air, she quickly came up with a plan that would free her. The fish told the Jaguar that if he'd release him back into the water, she'd let the Jaguar eat small parts of her for the rest of his life, that way, he'd never have to look for food again.

Since the Jaguar was easily fooled, he agreed and released the fish back into the river, who swam away as fast as he could, leaving the Jaguar hungry.

The Jaguar felt sad, and so he rushed to his friend, the Fox.

"If you spare me some meat today, I'll let you eat in peace tomorrow." Said the hungry Jaguar.

"Go away!" Shouted the furious Fox.

"I tried to look for food as you said I should, but the food fooled me and ran away!" Cried the Jaguar.

The Fox started laughing and asked, "How can food fool you? That doesn't make any sense."

The Jaguar shortly explained what had happened, and the Fox laughed harder!

"I'll spare you some meat, but tomorrow, you'll have to let me eat in peace!" Said Fox.

"Thank you, Fox!" Said the Jaguar

The Jaguar was so hungry, so much that he ate the meat in a few seconds. The Fox didn't judge the Jaguar since she knew he hadn't eaten for a few days. After eating, the Jaguar went back to his Cave and rested.

The morning after, the Jaguar was woken up by the Fox as she screeched, "Wake up lazy bones! Remember, today you'll have to look for your own food! I won't spare any!"

The Fox immediately flew away.

The Jaguar woke up and thought, "What shall I eat today? It seems like a nice day to eat a big plate of meat!" and so the Jaguar decided to go hunting.

As he was walking through the forest, the scorching sun made him tired and sweaty, and so the Jaguar decided to rest under a shade for a few minutes while thinking of a plan.

The Jaguar came up with a plan and went hunting the deers in the South of the river. After arriving, he hid behind a large tree and waited for a deer to pass by. After waiting a few hours, a deer finally showed up.

"Hello Deer, If you let me eat your leg, I won't disturb you ever again." Said the silly Jaguar.

After the deer heard the Jaguar, he ran as fast as he could. Jaguar sat and wondered, "Was I wrong? Isn't this how the Fox hunts! Then Why didn't the deer let me eat him!"

Other Deers passed by, and the Jaguar repeated the same question, yet they all ran away.

Jaguar was overwhelmed with sadness because,once again, he had failed to find food for himself.

The Sun fell away, and it was nighttime. The hungry Jaguar went to the Fox and told him what had happened! The Fox laughed and laughed!

"This is the last time I let you borrow my food, from today, you'll have to find your own food!" says the Fox as he gives him a plate of meat.

The Jaguar was starving. He finished the plate hastily and began licking it.

"I'll find my own food tomorrow! I promise. Thank you, my friend, for helping me during these times of need." Said the Jaguar.

As the Jaguar woke up the next day, the sky wasn't deep blue, the sun didn't rise, and Sunny hill was covered in darkness. As soon as the Jaguar saw this, he got worried.

"But how will I find food if there is no light!" the Jaguar thought to himself.

"I won't give up. I'll still find a way!" The Jaguar thought to himself.

The Jaguar went to look for food, but it was very dark, and he couldn't see anything.

Once again, the Jaguar wasn't successful at finding food.

The Jaguar was angry at himself for not hunting the day before and thought about asking the Fox for food.

Immediately after, he saw a shadow in the sky. It was the Fox!

"Fox! Fox! If you spare me some meat, I'll bring you food to eat tomorrow so you won't have to hunt!" The Jaguar said.

"Go and find your own food!", Replied the Fox.

"B-b-but I can't!" The Jaguar Hesitated.

"Why not? You are strong and fast!" Said Fox.

"My eyesight! The sun hasn't risen, I can't see, but your eyes are better than mine in the dark!" Said the Jaguar helplessly.

The Fox felt pity for the Jaguar, and so she said.

" The Sun isn't in the sky because it's in a box. The box is in a village in the west. The people in the Village open the box and let out the Sun, but they have stopped."

The Jaguar was surprised and said, "Is that so, what is your solution then?"

"Let's go to the Village and see the people with the sun, they will let out more light, and you will find your own food." Said Fox.

"Alright then! When does the journey begin?" Asked the Jaguar.

"It begins now!" Fox replied.

The two animals traveled together to the village in the west.

Jaguar's stomach grumbled throughout the Journey.

"Can you please look for food? I'm hungry?" Said the Jaguar.

"Alright, but after this journey, you'll have to look for your own food!" Said the Fox as she flew away looking for food.

After a short while, the Fox came back with a few fish. The two animals sought shelter in a cave, ate the fish, and went to sleep.

The next day, the Sun didn't rise. The Jaguar felt helpless.

"Don't worry, Jaguar, once we arrive at the Village and explain to them what's going on. You'll find the help you need. It will be alright!" Said Fox.

The two animals got up and continued their journey. To cheer up Jaguar, Fox kept making jokes.

"Why didn't the skeleton go to the party?" Asked the Fox.

"Why?" Jaguar boringly replied.

"Because he had no-body to go with! Get it? No-body?" Said the Fox as she laughed.

Jaguar didn't laugh, which was unusual since he was always funny and behaved foolishly.

"Thanks for trying, but I don't want to laugh, I just

want the sun to rise and to know how to find my own food." Said the sad Jaguar.

"I'll teach you, and the Sun will rise! Don't worry about it." Said Fox.

The Journey was long and left them feeling very tired. They hoped to arrive at the Village soon. Shortly after, they reached their destination.

To their surprise, there was a festival in the Village. They noticed that the dancers had a beautiful box, and each time they opened it, lovely rays of sunlight came out.

"That's the box of sunlight! We need to ask the villagers for some light." Said Fox.

"Of course not! We need to take the box!" Said the Jaguar.

The Fox wasn't pleased with the idea; all he wanted was a little light to help Jaguar find his own food.

The Villagers were generous and offered the Fox and Jaguar a delicious meal and a warm bed to sleep in.

"The Villagers are very good people; we shouldn't repay them by taking away their box!" Said Fox.

"What if they refuse to give us some light! What will we do? Will you let me starve?" Asked the Jaguar.

"I'll fly towards the box and take it. As soon as I have it on my Talons, we need to leave this village as fast as possible before the villagers find out." Said Fox.

Before the crack of dawn, when everyone was

asleep, Jaguar woke up the Fox. The Fox flew at the speed of light and took the box. Jaguar ran as fast as he could to catch up to the Fox, then the two went back home as quickly as possible. A villager noticed the box was missing and called the rest of the villagers, who began searching for their box.

In the middle of their journey, the curious Jaguar wanted to open the box, but the Fox told him to wait until they arrived at Sunny Hill.

"Wait until we arrive home, then you can open the box!" Said Fox.

"Why can't I open the box right now?" asked the Jaguar.

"B-b-because...Ah! Forget it! Just trust me." Said Fox.

"Are you hiding something from me?" Asked the Jaguar.

"Not at all! But if you want to open the box now. Don't open it quickly." Said Fox.

Jaguar was curious and didn't want to wait or listen to Fox's advice. Fox noticed this and flew far away and watched Jaguar from a distance.

The Jaguar opened the box quickly.

The Sun flew out—it looked like a giant ball of fire. It flew high up in the sky, but instead of the Earth becoming warm and bright, it became very dark and cold.

The flowers and trees shed their leaves and died.

The water bodies, rivers, and lakes turned into ice. Snowflakes began falling from the sky, covering Earth in soft white snow.

The Jaguar had made his first winter!

Every animal got to experience the beauty of winter. The Jaguar also had to learn how to take care of himself. He realized his laziness and lack of patience made him unhappy, so he vowed to change his behavior.

Made in United States
North Haven, CT
09 February 2022

15945461R00087